HER TWO DOMS

Ashe Barker

Cover design by www.studioenp.com

2nd print edition June 2020

With thanks to Karen and April, my fabulous beta readers who make all my stories so much better

And to Emmy Ellis, at www.studioenp - my wonderful editor and cover artist

I love to hear from my readers. Please feel free to follow me on social media.

Or you can email me direct on ashe.barker1@gmail.com

Better still, sign up for my newsletter to be the first to hear about new releases, competitions, giveaways and other fun stuff. You'll find the link on my website : www.ashebarker.com

Dreams can come true...

Ellie has adored Declan Stone and Iain Frazer-Lyons since she was twelve years old. Her schoolgirl crush was cut cruelly short when she made a disastrous mistake, but though they've all gone their separate ways her love for her 'golden boys' has never diminished. Now Iain (Fraze to his friends) is the Duke or Erskine, one of the richest and most successful businessmen in the country. Declan Stone is a top flight international footballer. There's no reason, none at all, why they should remember the geeky little kid who trailed after them at school.

But a chance meeting changes everything. Is it possible, after all these years, that her dreams might still come true? Might she actually be able to have both of these gorgeous men as Her Two Doms...?

CHAPTER ONE

When will I ever learn?

For someone with an IQ that allegedly qualifies me for membership of Mensa, I'm an expert at making the same mistake over and over. Case in point, my so-called overnight bag. It weighs as much as a small car. I stagger along the endless concrete walkway making up platform seven at Kings Cross station, heaving what must be half my worldly goods behind me on a pair of tiny wheels which scream for mercy. At least I'm travelling first class, one of the perks of heading up an international research team making ground-breaking progress on treatments for migraine. The condition blighted my childhood, but these days I can't complain. It's brought me fame and prestige within the world of medical research and put me very much in demand on the conference circuit. As head of the research team, I get paraded out to fly the flag. It's one of the conditions of my job, so I can grumble all I like, it's still happening.

But I do get to travel first class, so I reach my carriage a good ten minutes before I would have if I'd had to haul my case right down to the standard-class portion of the train. I check my ticket and the number embossed beside the door of the Virgin express headed for Edinburgh. This is me. I drag my luggage up the two small steps onto the train, then navigate the narrow corridor in search of my seat. I asked the department secretary to book me a forward-facing window seat so that should –

Bugger!

Seat twenty-seven in carriage B is a rear-facing aisle seat. I double check, but there it is, plain as you like. Still, the seat opposite, number twenty-five, is unoccupied. I check the overhead display and find that, like mine, seat number twenty-five has also been booked from Kings Cross to Edinburgh Waverley. The difference is, though, I'm here on the train and the rightful occupant of seat number twenty-five is not. The train is due to leave in less than two minutes, so perhaps… Anyway, I'll move if they show up.

I really should stow my case in the rack above my head, but I'd probably break my neck trying to lift it up there. Even with my laptop and notes safely tucked away in my briefcase, which doubles as a handbag, that still leaves clothes, shoes, toiletries, make up, and of course several books crammed into my case. I absolutely could not contemplate leaving my apartment without stuffing my bag with everything I could think of that I might conceivably need. There's no way I'm manhandling all that lot up into the overhead locker. It's all I can do to lift it onto the seat next to the aisle while I settle into the roomy window seat. I stretch out my legs, sink back against the plush upholstery, and heave a satisfied sigh of contentment as the inter-city express glides noiselessly out of the station.

We're off.

I like trains. Even though I could have made this trip in a fraction of the time if I'd flown to Edinburgh, I loathe airports. I especially dislike Heathrow, the airport closest to my flat in Richmond in West London. I appreciate the need for security, but everything about air travel is too frantic, too manic for my taste, and totally intimidating. These days there are armed police everywhere. I prefer the relative peace of a mainline station. So now, cocooned in the comfortable carriage I seem to have to myself, I can settle in for the next five hours or so and quite literally let the world go by.

I set up my laptop on the table in front of me and stretch my legs out under it. At five foot seven, I value plenty of leg room, another reason I love to travel first class. I pull up my conference notes and make a few, not especially necessary tweaks to the presentation I'll be giving tomorrow.

No less than two hundred leading academics will be assembled to hear about our latest insights on patient-centred and cost-effective management of migraine.

It's a talk I've rehearsed several times already. I know my material, can recite the statistics and analyse the data almost in my sleep. But this audience will be demanding, their questions more searching and critical. If there are any undefended areas in my reasoning, any aspect of my research not thoroughly and indisputably evidenced, I can be certain they will attack with military precision. I may be the best in my field, but I will be in good company tomorrow. The International Symposium on Clinical Excellence and Innovation is a big deal. The biggest. This has to be right.

I barely notice when the train begins to slow down. I'm engrossed in my work and only vaguely aware that we have stopped. Peterborough is the first port of call on this cross-country journey, and a couple of people make their way down the central corridor to disembark. I ignore them as I scan the rows of figures in my data tables, checking for any stray anomaly or inconsistency that might be seized upon tomorrow.

"Twenty-nine, twenty-eight, twenty-seven…right, this is us."

Male voices reach me, but still I ignore them. I have no interest in my fellow passengers. It's only when a bright orange holdall is dumped unceremoniously on the table next to my laptop that I look up and meet his gaze.

And I freeze.

Declan Stone.

My breath hitches in my throat. I remember those dark-grey eyes. I remember them with infinite clarity despite not having seen them for seventeen years. I'd know Declan Stone anywhere, although he's filled out somewhat from the rangy fourteen-year-old I knew back at St. Hugh's College in Hexham, Northumberland. He was heart-stoppingly gorgeous then and is even more so now. I goggle at him in disbelief. Can it really be…?

"I think this is my seat." Declan Stone consults the ticket in his hand. "Yup, twenty-six. This one." He indicates the seat currently occupied by my ridiculously heavy case.

"Oh, right. I'm sorry, I—"

"Well, which is mine, then? Twenty-five?" Another large male shoulders Declan to one side as he leans in to inspect the seat numbers, and my heart is definitely about to give up the ghost.

If there was one boy at St Hugh's who was even more attractive than Declan Stone, it had to be Iain Frazer-Lyons. The pair of them were inseparable then and seem to be just as tight all these years later, although I know their lives have taken completely different courses. I watch the news, I know what they've both been up to these past several years. Yet here they are, together, on a train bound for Edinburgh.

And I'm in their seats. Both of them.

"I'm sorry, I thought these were spare." I start to fold up my laptop. "They were reserved from Kings Cross, and when the train pulled out and they were still empty I thought—"

"Ah, yes. We decided to get on at Peterborough instead." Iain Frazer-Lyons' soft Scottish brogue is every bit as sexy as it ever was. "Hey, let me help you with that." He takes hold of the handle of my case and hauls it from the seat alongside me. "I can put it up there if you like. Unless you need anything out of it…?"

"What? No, I don't need anything. It's heavy, though, so—"

He just grins, a smile which used to melt my insides back in the day and now just melts my knickers instead. He starts to lift it, then flashes me an amused look. "Hey, do you have a body in here?"

"No, only—"

"Give me a hand, will you?" Iain glares at Declan. "Don't just stand there."

Between the pair of them, my case is soon hoisted up and into the locker. Flustered and embarrassed, I start to scramble out of the seat ready to move into the one rightfully allocated to me.

"No, you stay where you are. I'll sit here." Iain drops into the seat opposite and treats me to that gorgeous smile again. To my horror, Declan slides in beside me, taking the place previously occupied by my bag. I'm trapped, sandwiched between them. For the next four hours.

"So, Miss…?" Iain pauses, inviting me to tell him my name.

My heart sinks, crumbles. They don't recognise me. I have their images indelibly etched on my consciousness, and these two don't remember me at all.

Iain waits, one aristocratic blond eyebrow raised, his moss-green eyes courteously expectant. I can only stare across the narrow table at him, a butterfly pinned in the brilliant glow of his aura. His features were always impeccable, I was wonderstruck back then and the magic hasn't faded. His strong jaw, finely chiselled nose, expensively styled ash-blond hair, and enticingly agile mouth create a picture of perfection, the product of centuries of flawless breeding, privilege, and a lineage which can be traced back to Robert the Bruce.

Iain clears his throat. "My name's Iain. The lout next to you is Dec."

I know.

"And you are…?"

His smile is pleasant enough, encouraging.

At last I find my voice. "Eleanor. Eleanor Davidson."

It's embarrassment. That and pure, abject humiliation which makes me give them my married name. They shouldn't have to ask. They should know me, instantly, as I know them. But they don't, they forgot all about me, and that hurts. I could have offered the name they might recognise, the name I was known by at school, but I prefer to spare us all the inevitable awkwardness as they realise their mistake and fall over themselves in their efforts to apologise. There's no reason they should connect Eleanor Davidson to little Ellie Scott, the skinny, bespectacled twelve-year-old who followed them around the school like a lost puppy for half a term.

"Eleanor. Yes, that suits you. Very classy. Are you going all the way to Edinburgh?"

"Yes," I reply. "Yes, Edinburgh."

"Business or pleasure?" asks Declan, seated beside me.

"Business. A conference."

Declan gives a short nod. "Oh. What conference is that?"

"It's about clinical research."

"I see. Is that your field, then? Are you a clinical researcher?"

"Yes, I am. I… I'm giving a keynote speech."

I don't know why I add the final bit. Vanity I suppose, and a lingering desire to impress these two. Anyway, it seems to do the trick with Iain Frazer-Lyons. He nods his approval. "I see. What's your topic?"

"Migraine."

He inclines his head again and seems to want to know more. "Important stuff. So, what are you going to be saying about migraine?"

"I…my team in Imperial College has been working on migraine pathophysiology…"

Both men exchange a bemused look.

I try to translate into layman's language. "That's what happens in the brain to cause migraine attacks. We're working on techniques to slow the development of migraine and maybe prevent attacks altogether. Drugs aren't right for everyone— pregnant women, for example, or patients with other complicating conditions. So my team has been working on non-drug options. The results are very promising and…there's a lot of interest."

Declan twists in his seat to better regard me. "I imagine there is."

"I was working when you got on. I have things I need to finish, to check before tomorrow, so if you don't mind, I'll… I need to carry on…"

"Oh?" Declan regards me with amusement. "But you closed down your laptop."

"Yes, but I have to…" I grab it and pull it back in front of me, then flip open the lid. I turn to look at Declan. "Would you like to swap places? Then you can talk to Iain…I mean to your friend."

"Iain's fine," confirms the man himself. "But we're okay. You stay where you are and do your…whatever. I'm going to get a coffee from the buffet car. Would you like anything?"

"No, thank you. And anyway, someone will come round soon to take orders."

"I want my coffee now." Iain Frazer-Lyons eases himself along and out into the aisle. "Are you sure I can't interest you?"

Interest me? You fucking fascinate me. You always did. "No, really," I mutter. "I'm fine."

"I'll have an espresso if they do that. Otherwise just a normal black coffee." Declan gives his order then settles back with that lopsided, mischievous grin I remember so well. "Run along, then."

It's a piece of banter which throws me straight back to when we were at school together, a private joke between the pair of them. Iain offers his friend a one-finger salute, then saunters off along the corridor in the direction of the buffet car.

With Iain gone, I have a few minutes in which to take in Declan Stone. Declan is every bit as handsome as Iain, though the two are not remotely similar in appearance. Where Iain is blond and beautiful, Declan is dark and brooding. His hair is a rich ebony shade, cropped short now, though it used to be much longer. He has the toned, athletic build of the professional sportsman I know him to be.

I take advantage of the respite to start up my laptop and lean forward to peer intently at the screen. It's no use. The figures in my tables dance in front of my eyes. My concentration is shattered. In my mind I'm back there, a shy, lonely twelve-year-old sent away to school, desperately homesick and completely out of her depth. No wonder, then, that I latched on to the first people to show me the least bit of interest. Just my luck that they happened to be Iain Frazer-Lyons, known as Fraze to his friends from the rugby club and the cricket first eleven, and Declan Stone, top scorer in the school soccer team.

Declan and Fraze were something of a legend at St. Hugh's, a charmed duo who could do no wrong. They excelled at everything and were easily the most popular boys among staff and students alike. No wonder I was mesmerised by them.

I got into St. Hugh's on a scholarship. I was one of the lucky few awarded places in a government initiative to drive up standards in science, technology, engineering, and mathematics. They invited entries from comprehensive schools, and I was put forward because I was good at maths and sciences. It was, I daresay, one of the few occasions when being a female actually worked to my advantage... positive discrimination and all that. Anyway, I was offered the coveted place at one of the north of England's most prestigious independent schools where my talent was, presumably, to be honed and polished. My parents were ecstatic, even if it did mean I'd be away at school for thirty weeks a year.

My dad worked for Leeds Council in the Libraries department, and my mum was on the checkouts at Tesco.

There was no way they could have afforded a private education for me, and they were always going to struggle to put me through university, too, though I know they intended to shift Heaven and Earth to make it happen. The scholarship was my passport to all that they wanted for me and more.

So off I went, a fresh-faced, enthusiastic, apprehensive eleven-year-old from inner city Leeds, thrust out there alone among the flower of English and Scottish youth. The only problem was, I knew no one. I spoke with a broad Yorkshire accent, had no idea about correct table manners or how to properly address a bishop. My parents drove me up to St. Hugh's in their seven-year-old Ford Fiesta, whilst my classmates swanned through the great iron gates in Daimlers and Alfa Romeos. I arrived with two changes of uniform, my sports kit in a gym bag made for me by my grandmother, and five pounds spending money. My parents promised to send me more in a couple of weeks or so, if I needed it.

My classmates wore designer clothes and top-of-the-range sportswear. They had accounts at the various stores in the city and as much cash as they needed. They swapped tales of holidays in the Bahamas or the Seychelles and whined about Daddy's latest posting to New York or Moscow and the problems of finding a half-decent gamekeeper these days.

For the first few weeks I spoke to almost no one. I attended my classes and did the work the teachers asked of me. I did my best, and the work wasn't especially difficult, so I expected no issues as far as that was concerned. But there were. It soon became apparent that I was rather better at mathematics than the rest of the students in my year group, and several parents complained that I was undermining their little princelings' confidence. The head teacher decided to move me up a year, and then another when a similar issue arose again. I found myself in classes with students two years my senior, and still I more than held my own. I felt like an oddity, some sort of freak. I was set apart by much more than my modest background.

Then I met Fraze and Declan.

I was put in the same class as them for mathematics and physics, subjects in which neither of them possessed the slightest aptitude.

I suppose my fame preceded me, because the first morning when I sidled into the classroom, intending to settle down at the back, out of sight, Declan shouted to me across the room.

"Hey, Einstein. Come over and sit with us."

I ignored him. He was obviously not talking to me. I headed for the rear row of seats.

Declan leapt up and darted across to meet me before I could sit down. "We saved you a seat. Over here." He grabbed my elbow and firmly led me back to where Fraze waited.

Dumbstruck, I dropped into the spare seat and plonked my bag on the floor next to me.

"So, we can't keep calling you Einstein. I'm Fraze and he's Declan. You're Ellie, right?"

"Er, yes. How did you…?"

Fraze just offered me his glowing smile, and my questions ceased. These two knew everything, everyone. I waited, miserable, knowing they had brought me over here to make fun of me somehow. It seemed all the more cruel, coming from them, these god-like creatures.

But they didn't. They were nice. They were good company and generous. Fraze—Iain Frazer-Lyons—was heir to the Duke of Erskine, rich as Croesus and lined up to inherit most of the Highlands and Western Isles as far as I could make out. Declan was his friend, the son of the duke's housekeeper. The two had grown up together on the vast estate, and Fraze's father insisted they attend the same school so he was paying the fees for both. Declan displayed not a shred of servility despite the difference in their station in life, nor did Fraze seem to expect it. They were equals, inseparable, and merciless in their teasing of each other. Declan would order Fraze about, and Fraze would call him a peasant. Neither took the slightest offence, it was just the way it was with them. From their behaviour on the train it would seem not a lot had changed.

They took me under their wing somehow, and my life at St. Hugh's was transformed. I found myself eating with them in the huge refectory and soon learnt the rudiments of posh table manners.

I would watch them playing their respective sports, seated next to Fraze at soccer matches or with Declan as we clapped politely and congratulated Fraze's batting prowess when he hit yet another six.

Because I was in their exalted orbit, I bathed in the reflected glow and found a new acceptance among the other students. I was still shy, still awestruck, but less lonely now because I was part of the social fabric of St Hugh's.

All of this came at a price, of course, and it was one I was happy to pay. I helped them with their prep, coached them before exams, went over the notes from our lessons again and again to help them to understand what the teacher had tried but utterly failed to get across.

"We both fucked up maths for the last two years," explained Fraze. "My father will insist on a private tutor if I don't manage to get a decent grade this time, and that'll put a stop to me going on a rugby tour in New Zealand. That's not happening, so we're relying on you, Ellie, to get us through the exam."

"Of course," I replied. "I'd love to help you."

All went well. I tutored them in prep, and in return I became the envy of every girl at St Hugh's. I was scrawny, wore cheap National Health glasses and chain store clothes, but I was accepted because Fraze and Declan made it clear I was part of their crowd. Life was good, and I was happy.

Then, disaster struck. Lawrence Mortimer, another boy in our year and one not known for either integrity or honesty, broke into the office of the head of maths and photocopied the exam paper which we were all to sit the following week. For a mere hundred pounds each he would sell a copy of the paper to anyone who fancied a sneak preview.

Naturally, he offered the deal to Fraze. And naturally, having been brought up to do the right and honourable thing, Fraze refused.

But I had other ideas. I knew how vital the exam was to Fraze, and I also knew the likelihood of him passing with a decent grade was pretty slim, however much I coached him. Declan was marginally better at quadratic equations, but there wasn't much to pick between them. That stolen exam paper could make all the difference.

"I could work through the paper, and you could copy my answers. All you'd need to do is remember them for the exam. You'd get at least some right, enough to pass, surely."

"It's cheating," Fraze pointed out unnecessarily. "We could get expelled for this."

"Not as long as your father's footing the bill for the new gymnasium," I replied. "And anyway, we're not going to get caught. I'll run through the questions, work out the answers and let you copy my paper. Simple."

Fraze had his doubts, Declan, too. I waved away their worries. "Everyone cheats if they can, it's just the way it is. Come on, let's go find Lawrence Mortimer."

I'm not a naturally deceitful person. I wasn't then, either. I would never had dreamed of cheating in an exam for my own benefit—never had to—but I was so completely dazzled by Fraze and Declan, and so desperate to remain indispensable to them, that I was ready to do anything to make sure nothing changed. I was under their spell somehow, so I squashed my own conscience, ignored their objections, and did what I thought needed to be done.

Declan and I waited behind the cricket pavilion while Fraze bought the paper from Lawrence, then the three of us headed for the small double room they shared. Soon I was leafing through the exam paper, making notes and working out the various problems and calculations. It was easy enough, and I'd have had no trouble at all in the exam a few days later, sneak preview or not. When I finished, I let them have my notes from the cribbed exam paper.

By now both boys had managed to overcome their finer feelings on the matter. Fraze scanned the pages then hugged me. Declan swung me around until my glasses flew off, then he grinned as he helped me retrieve them.

"You're a star," he declared. "Brains and beauty, what a combination."

I was ecstatic and remained so—for all of twenty-four hours. By then the maths tutor had noticed that his office had been robbed and made some enquiries. Lawrence Mortimer was soon identified as the culprit, and he took little persuading to expose the other students who had bought the copied paper. Fraze was hauled in to see the head teacher, and Declan, too, of course, since they were known to do everything together.

I waited in the dormitory I shared with seven other girls. It was only a matter of time before the head master sent for me, too.

My father carried no influence with the board of governors. He wasn't paying for a new library wing or upgrading the swimming pool, and in any case, I had been the ringleader. Fraze and Declan would never have approached Lawrence Mortimer but for me. We'd all be in trouble, but they would probably scrape by with a telling off and disqualification from the exam. Me? I'd be expelled for certain.

St. Hugh's hadn't exactly embraced the scholarship concept with enthusiasm, and this would be their excuse to be rid of me. They'd say I most likely cheated on my exams before, that I didn't truly deserve the place in their prestigious school. I'd be sent back to my comprehensive in Leeds, in disgrace. My parents would be mortified, ashamed of me. Deeply honest and hard-working themselves, they wouldn't even start to understand why I'd done such a thing. As I sat, quivering, on my narrow bunk, I was hard pressed to understand it, either.

But no one came. No stern-faced prefect appeared at the door with a message requiring me to attend the head master's office. I didn't dare tempt fate by venturing out and asking what was going on, so I stayed in the dorm and pretended to be ill. The school nurse came to see me, could find nothing to alarm her so let me stay where I was. The kitchen sent my evening meal up to me and my breakfast the next morning. By then I decided I would draw more attention by continuing to hide than by rejoining mainstream school life, so I went to the refectory at lunchtime and found a seat as far as I could from the table I normally shared with Fraze and Declan.

They were there, in the dining hall, and even from the other end of the room I could tell that both looked very subdued. I later found out that the trip to New Zealand was cancelled and that both of them were condemned to spend every evening and weekend until the end of term cleaning the school toilets and showers. Naturally, they were both deemed to have failed the exam.

"It was you, wasn't it? You helped those two with the maths paper," Phoebe Watson Fforbes whispered to me across the table.

"Who says I did? What have you heard?"

She shrugged. "Just that Fraze and Dec were caught cheating, and that someone helped them to do the maths paper. Everyone knows it was you. Who else could it have been?"

"How should I know? It was nothing to do with me," I lied. I was convinced the entire school was watching me, listening to my falsehoods. Even now, after so many years have passed, I can still feel the heat that rose up from my neck as I flushed, the very picture of guilt.

Phoebe just smirked at me. "Okay, okay. Who cares, anyway? So, tell me, is Fraze a good kisser…?"

I glared at her, refusing to answer as I busied myself with my semolina pudding. Phoebe gave up. But she knew. They all knew…

But no one else ever confronted me with my crime. I sat the exam the following week and did well, of course, though I took no pride in it. The sneak preview made no difference, I'd have aced it anyway, but even so…

By mutual but unspoken consent, I stayed well away from Declan and Fraze from then on. I no longer sat with them, stopped attending the sports events, ate my meals with Lucinda mostly, though she bored me with her constant chatter about cosmetics and fashion.

Although we never spent time together any more, I knew when Fraze and Declan left St Hugh's and I missed them desperately. Declan got a place in the Newcastle United Academy and was on the road to becoming a professional footballer. He was playing on their first team by the time he was seventeen and joined the Scotland international squad two years later. Most of his playing career was spent in Spain, though I saw on the news that he recently transferred back to play for a club in the English First Division.

Fraze's career has been less in the public eye. The Duke of Erskine died in a freak skiing accident, and Frazer inherited the title when he was just twenty. I read somewhere that he studied law at university, and, despite his lack of mathematical aptitude, has proven in the decade or so since to be adept at financial management. He's one of the wealthiest men in the country, and if the Financial Times is to be believed, has elevated his position on that league by several places since he took over the Erskine estates.

Neither of my childhood heroes has ever married—I'd have spotted that little snippet had it occurred.

Declan was involved with an American model for a while, but they had a rather public split when she took it into her empty, but extremely pretty head, to sleep with the team captain in Barcelona. Idiot woman! As for Fraze, I never heard or read anything to associate him with either a specific woman or any scandal. His father would have been very proud.

CHAPTER TWO

I manage to make a decent show of ignoring Declan as I pretend to be absorbed in my work. He soon abandons any attempt to engage me in conversation and resorts to studying his iPhone. A sneaky sideways glance tells me he's actually reading an ebook rather than playing Candy Crush Saga. Whatever, it keeps him occupied until Iain returns with one of those small paper bags the train services hand out for carrying drinks.

Iain places an espresso in front of Declan and a tall latte in his own place. He also produces a bottle of water from the bag and sets that down beside my laptop.

"I know you said you didn't want anything, but it's a long journey, so I thought…"

I gaze across the table at him as he retakes his seat. He dazzles me, again, with that gorgeous smile. Still nice, still generous, still thoughtful and kind to those around him, even a not especially polite stranger on a train.

"Thank you," I mutter. "Next time I'll go and get the drinks."

"Okay." He takes an experimental sip of his coffee. "How's the work going?"

"Oh…fine." I drag my gaze back to the screen and pretend to be studying the data displayed there. "I'm sorry, I don't mean to be rude, but…"

"No problem." Iain settles back to admire the view of southern England as it hurtles past outside. "Don't let us disturb you."

The next hour or so passes in silence, more or less.

We are disturbed only by the ticket inspection and a brief stop at Newark. More passengers get on, and one youngster travelling with his father recognises Declan. The man looks sheepish and apologises for disturbing us, but could his son have an autograph, please?

Declan obliges, scrawling his signature on one of the napkins which came with the coffee, then agrees to the ubiquitous selfie, too. He chats with the lad for a few minutes before the father, clearly embarrassed but grateful for the attention, drags the boy away to their seats.

I'm not certain what to say. In creating the impression that I haven't met my fellow passengers before, I'm not supposed to know that Declan is a footballer with an international career, an icon for every budding David Beckham. Neither can I reasonably ignore what just happened. It's not every day that perfect strangers ask for an autograph. I'm spared having to deal with the issue when Iain chuckles.

"Christ, you kick a lump of leather about, score a goal or two, and suddenly you're a fucking superhero."

"Ah," I murmur, seizing on the opening, "you play football." As if I didn't know…

"Yeah." Declan smirks at Iain, and this time it's he who offers the single-finger salute. He turns to me. "Please excuse my companion's language. He's jealous because no one ever asks him for a selfie, and because women prefer me, too."

Iain merely laughs at that. "Talking of women, how's the beautiful Allannah these days?"

"She's well, except that she always complains when I don't go to see her while I'm in Scotland."

I rack my brains and recall that Allannah is the name of Declan's mother, the housekeeper to the duke.

"If you do get there I might come with you and beg her to come back to Hatfield with me." Iain grins at his friend. "I could offer to marry her," he adds hopefully.

"You can forget that. My mother's retired now and done skivvying for you posh dickheads and she certainly wouldn't fancy marrying one. She's having a fine time living in her little cottage, playing crown green bowling and breeding cairn terriers. She hardly has time to take my phone calls let alone mop up after you."

Iain shrugs. "Pity. This new woman we hired is okay, but she doesn't have Allannah's touch with pastry."

"Get used to it," snarls Declan, then returns to his ebook.

I've been trying to give the impression I'm not listening, that I'm not in the least interested in their conversation. Declan might be prepared to let me continue with my little fantasy but not Iain, it seems. He leans across the table to offer me a mint. I'm about to decline but at the last moment I decide I do quite fancy one.

"Thank you." I pop it in my mouth and savour the sudden, sharp burst of peppermint before returning to my work.

Iain decides to strike up another conversation. "So, do you suffer from migraines, Eleanor? Is that why you chose to research it?"

I shake my head. "No, not any more, though I used to as a child. It was something that interested me and it affects a lot of people."

Iain nods. "My cousin used to suffer from migraines, too. They were triggered by eating too much chocolate."

"No they weren't," I retort without thinking. "That's a common myth."

He raises one blond eyebrow. "I beg your pardon?"

"A craving for sweet foods and chocolate is common at the start of an attack, and many people associate eating the chocolate, say, with the migraine that follows. It's a symptom not a cause."

"I see. I must remember to mention this to Fiona."

"You could send her a Godiva gift box," suggests Declan without even looking up from his phone. "No, better still, I will. Maybe I'll give her a call, too, while I'm here."

"Dream on, bro. You might as well save your money. Fiona never much liked you."

"Yes she did!" Declan regards Iain under his dark eyebrows. "She almost let me kiss her in the stables one time when she was staying at Hathersmuir."

"Liar. You probably sneaked up on her and she was too kind-hearted to kick you in the nuts as you deserved. No problem, I'd be happy to do it for her. Anyway, I doubt she'd let you kiss her now, and her husband certainly wouldn't."

"That accountant of hers?" Declan gives a derisory snort. "Fiona married him on the rebound. It won't last."

"Adrian's a director of the Bank of England, and they've been married for eight years. They have two little girls. Fiona adores him, as you well know."

Declan shrugs. "If you say so." He turns to me, his expression pleasant and deceptively calm. "Eleanor, if I tried to kiss you, would you try to kick me in the nuts?"

"What?" I gape at him. "What did you just say?"

He turns back to Iain who is scowling from across the table. "See, Eleanor agrees. She wouldn't have kicked me in the nuts and neither would Fiona. I think maybe I'll just drop your lovely cousin a text…"

"You've embarrassed our companion." Iain bestows his smile on me again. "You must forgive my uncouth friend. He had a deprived childhood and as a result experiences difficulty controlling his delusional tendencies. He's further hampered by total lack of anything that might pass for manners. It's really very sad. Perhaps you could find a cure for him—after you've finished with the migraine, obviously."

I'm speechless. Caught in the middle of their banter, it's as though I'm twelve years old all over again. I shake my head. "I'm sorry, I don't…"

"See? Now who's embarrassed our companion?" Declan stretches out his long legs as he leans back in his seat. "You're only jealous because our gorgeous Ms Davidson doesn't want to kiss you."

"Of course she does, though neither me nor the lovely Eleanor are given to public displays of affection. It's the breeding…"

"In-breeding," corrects Declan.

Iain frowns at Declan. "How dare you insinuate such a thing about a perfectly respectable clinical researcher about to deliver a keynote speech. You absolutely should apologise to Eleanor."

"Oh, no," I interrupt. "Really, Fraze, there's no need…."

They both turn their stares on me, the one dark and stormy grey, the other a deep, brilliant emerald. Gone is the banter in an instant.

"What…?" I begin. "Why are you staring at me?"

"You called me Fraze." Iain's tone is soft, deceptively so. "How did you know that name?"

"I don't. I mean, it's just, since your surname is Frazer, and—"

"I never told you that. I told you my name was Iain, and that he was Declan. No surnames."

Caught out, I look from one to the other. Still I plough on. "I suppose Declan must have mentioned your full name…"

"No," Declan says quietly. "I didn't."

"Do we know you, Eleanor?" Iain studies me, his scrutiny long and searching. "I admit I thought you seemed familiar, something in the voice, perhaps…"

Declan shakes his head. "Not the voice. It's the eyes." He narrows his own dark-chocolate eyes and peruses me with care. "We do know you…"

I try to look away, lower my gaze back to the laptop, but Iain reaches across to cup my chin in his palm.

"Yes, you're right. The eyes…"

I know the moment realisation dawns.

"Holy fuck," he breathes. "It's Ellie. Little Ellie Scott."

Declan twists in his seat to stare at me. In my peripheral vision I can see him nodding. "Ellie Scott, as I live and breathe…"

Well and truly outed, I can only squirm in my seat and try not to flush crimson. At the latter, I fail utterly.

"Why didn't you say so? Why pretend not to know us? You obviously did recognise us, or you wouldn't have let it slip and called me Fraze just now."

"And what's with the name nonsense?" puts in Declan. "Who the fuck is Eleanor Davidson?"

"Me," I protest. "It…it's my married name. And I was always Eleanor, it was just usually shortened to Ellie."

"Married?" Declan repeats the word softly, one eyebrow raised.

"Yes. Briefly. I… I still use the name, though, professionally."

"I see. And where's Mr Davidson now?"

"In New Zealand. Raising sheep with his new wife and four step-children." I pause, then, "We…we wanted different things in life."

"It certainly sounds like it," agrees Declan. "Sheep, eh?"

"And four children?" adds Fraze.

I nod. "At the last count. It's been five years since I heard from him, so by now…"

Declan tilts his head to one side, assessing my revelations. "You didn't want kids, I assume?"

"Maybe. Eventually. But not fresh out of college when I'd just been offered a job in the Imperial College's Faculty of Medicine. It was exactly what I'd been working towards, my dream. Jerome wasn't prepared to wait, and I wasn't ready to compromise. We were both young, and selfish, I suppose. We went our separate ways. It…it was a relief, actually."

Iain leans back in his seat. "So, should we be calling you Eleanor or is it still Ellie to your friends?"

"Ellie will be fine," I whisper.

"You still haven't said why you didn't tell us straight away. You recognised us, didn't you? Right from the start?"

I nod.

"So," prompts Iain. "Why pretend you didn't?"

"B-because you didn't remember me, and I felt humiliated. I'd have known you two anywhere, but you'd forgotten all about me."

"No, we hadn't. It's just, you look…different."

Declan agrees. "You wore glasses back then, and your hair wasn't the same colour. And you weren't nearly so tall."

"Well, neither were you, but I still managed."

Iain frowns. "Fair point. So you were intending to let us travel all the way to Scotland and never let on that we went to school together? Is that about the size of it?"

"You make it sound as if I planned this. I had no idea you were going to get on the same train as me. But I was upset, caught on the back foot, and I acted on impulse."

"We didn't mean to upset you."

"But you did. You didn't recognise me. I was hurt…and I suppose I wondered if you did it on purpose. To get back at me for…for…"

"On purpose?" Declan glowers at me. "Why would we do that?"

"Because of that exam. At school. I got you into trouble…"

They look at each other, clearly bemused.

Iain shrugs. "Sorry, but you'll need to help us out here. What exam?"

"That time when I helped you to cheat." I swing my gaze from one to the other. How could they have forgotten? It was huge, easily the worst thing that ever happened to me during my entire childhood.

"Ah, right. I remember now. Lawrence What's-His-Face and the stolen exam paper." Declan's dark features split in a smile of genuine amusement as he grins at Iain. "You must remember, we got roasted by old Mr Hennessy and ended up scrubbing the toilets for fucking weeks."

Iain nods, also smiling. "Lawrence Mortimer. Shit, yes. I can still smell the disinfectant."

"I'm sorry," I begin. "It was all my fault."

"Was it?" Iain appears genuinely puzzled. "I always blamed that weasel Mortimer. He was the idiot who couldn't pull off a decent burglary, then went and told anyone who asked the names every student who bought his copies. There was quite a line of us outside Mr Hennessy's office, as I recall."

"You got in trouble, and it was all my idea. I persuaded you to do it."

"Did you?" Declan furrows his brow as he tries to recall the details. "You were younger than us, I remember that. And we liked having you about, you were useful when it came to doing our prep, but I don't think you had that much influence over us. Not really."

"I did," I insist. I recall the conversation perfectly. "Fraze said it would be cheating, and it was, but I didn't care. I talked you into going to find Lawrence and buying the paper from him, then I did the exam and gave you the right answers…"

Fraze shook his head. "I don't think we'd have done what you told us to do, not if we were really against it. Yes, we cheated, or tried to, and in pointing that out back then, if I did, I would have been just stating the obvious. I don't think we'd have been swayed by a kid so much younger, no matter how bright you were."

"Or how pretty," puts in Declan.

"Pretty? I wasn't pretty."

"Oh, but you were," insists Declan. "We both agreed on that. You were too young, though, so not girlfriend material. And we'd have fallen out over you. We'd have been fighting in the quad, knocking seven bells out of each other. Back in those days we hadn't learnt to share nicely."

I stare at him. My eyes must be the size of saucers. "Share nicely? What does that mean? Surely you don't share girlfriends…"

They exchange a look, but neither chooses to respond to my question. Instead, Iain—or Fraze as I prefer to think of him—returns to the matter of the stolen exam paper.

"Was that why you dumped us? Something to do with the cheating?"

"Alleged cheating," observes Declan. "We never actually sat the exam, so…"

"It was cheating," confirms Fraze. "We should be ashamed of ourselves. My father certainly thought so and pointed it out on a number of occasions, as did Mr Hennessy."

"He was the headmaster, he had to say that."

I can't believe that they would be so casually dismissive. For me, this incident remains the crime of the decade. "How can you joke about it? It was serious. We could all have been expelled."

Again, they exchange a glance. "Could we?" Fraze shrugs. "I never thought of it like that."

"Well, I did. I was terrified. I hid in my dormitory for a whole day, then I spent the rest of that term trying not to be noticed. I was sure Mr Hennessy was going to throw me out. And…and I lied about it when anyone asked."

"You lied about it?" He tuts to himself. Iain Frazer-Lyons is laughing at me but he's much too well bred to do it out loud.

I nod, deeply embarrassed and ashamed. "One of the other girls, Phoebe Watson Fforbes, asked me if I was the one who worked out the answers. I said I wasn't, but she didn't believe me. No one believed me, they all knew it must have been me."

Fraze isn't having that, seemingly. "Not everyone. They can't have, or you'd have been in Mr Hennessy's sights, too. We never mentioned your name to him."

"I realise that. I thought you must have kept quiet about my involvement but I couldn't work out why. It was my fault, my idea. You only had to tell them that, and—"

Declan reaches for me and lays his hand over mine. "Ellie, it wasn't your fault. Even if it was, we would never have told on you."

I blink at him but he just smiles and contoinues.

"Apart from anything, you had a scholarship to worry about. Our fees were paid, there was no way we'd be slung out. But you…"

"I know. That's why I lied and that's why I didn't dare to be your friend anymore. I was too scared that someone would connect me to what had happened. But it doesn't make it right."

"Well at least now we know why you dropped the pair of us like a hot brick. I confess, if there was anything that pissed me off, it was that."

"True enough," agrees Fraze. "Me, too. But stop beating yourself up, Ellie. It's done with. Over. We haven't given it a thought in years."

"I have, I feel awful about it still."

"There's no need…"

"How can you not be angry." I swing my gaze from Declan's darkly handsome features to Fraze's blond male beauty. "I left you to take the blame. I was a coward as well as a cheat."

"Ellie, you had a lot more to lose than we did." Fraze smiles at me. "You just said so yourself. You were right to be scared and to keep a low profile until it all blew over. As for being a cheat, that's rubbish. You had no need to cheat. You could have done that exam in your sleep."

"You're just being kind. Why can't you be angry? At least then I could apologise."

Declan shrugs. "Feel free to apologise if you really think that's necessary. Then we can all move on."

"But I can't," I whimper. "You were punished, and I wasn't. That wasn't right, it wasn't fair."

Fraze glances across at Declan. "Well, I doubt if Mr Hennessy has much call for toilet cleaners these days. I gather the old boy retired a few years back. I suppose we could let you buy us lunch…"

"I'll happily pay for lunch, but that hardly compares to weeks of disinfectant and scrubbing brushes."

"Perhaps not," acknowledges Fraze, "but it's the best we can do after all these years."

"I know." I hang my head and wonder how much longer it will be until we reach the next station. Maybe I could get off the train, catch the next one, and—

"Well, we could spank her, I suppose." Declan offers this solution as though it's the most normal thing in the world.

"Yes, I was wondering about that. A decent spanking might even out the scores a bit." Fraze flattens his gorgeous lips as though seriously considering this insane solution. "Yes, I think that might work."

"Bare bottom, obviously," adds Declan.

"Obviously. We could bend her over the table and take turns."

"Or she could lie across our laps. First me, then you…"

"How come you get to spank her first? I cleaned more toilets than you did."

"Bro, your memory's slipping. I blame it on poor genes. Still, we could toss a coin for it."

"Or we could let Ellie decide who goes first." Fraze nods, satisfied. "Yes, that's the best solution." They both turn to me. "How does that sound to you?"

I can only gape in utter bewilderment. These two were always inclined to catch me off guard, but today's madness trumps anything from our school days. I'm vaguely aware that my mouth is opening and closing as I search for words, any words that might constitute a sensible response. It's only when Declan reaches for my chin and firmly closes my jaw that I realise how goldfish-like I have become.

"We could toss for it, I suppose," offers Fraze.

Declan shrugs. "Fair enough. We're agreed, then?" He settles back in his seat. "I'm looking forward to this."

I find my voice, not before time. "No! No way. Are you both quite mad?"

"I don't think so," replies Fraze. "At least, I'm not mad. Are you mad, Dec?"

"Nope, not me. Perfectly calm."

"Mad, as in delusional," I clarify. "You can't just go around spanking women you meet on a train."

"We didn't meet you on a train. Well, we did, just now, but—"

I cut off Fraze's inane excuses. "I'm a grown woman, not some star-struck little girl you can push around like at school. A spanking? For Christ's sake, it's ridiculous. And on my bare bottom? That's…that's just perverted. It would be…sexual. And an assault."

I'm pinned in my seat by both their intent stares. Neither is grinning now, no one is joking anymore.

Declan starts. "You're right, at least on some counts. What we're suggesting is not at all like being at school, though I don't believe we pushed you around then, either. But you are indeed a grown woman, and this would be a grown-up spanking, between consenting adults. Yes, it could be sexual. Often is, but no one's about to force you into anything you really don't want to do."

"But—"

"And we would never assault you, sexually or otherwise. If this happens, it will be with your consent."

"Why would I ever consent to such a thing?" I whisper.

Fraze shrugs. "To deal with the lingering guilt. Or maybe because the idea excites you, intrigues you. Arouses you, even…?"

"Arouses me? That's ridiculous…"

Or would be, were my knickers not already dampening at the prospect of baring my bottom and bending over, of knowing that they're standing behind me, looking at my exposed pussy while they slap my buttocks. I clench, and the expression must be writ plain across my face as both now smile at me.

They know. They bloody well know!

"It's up to you, Ellie. Think about it. Imagine it. There's no harm in that."

"I don't… I mean, I—"

"Ah, here's the nice man from the buffet car come to take our order for lunch. Is your offer to pay still on, Ellie?" Declan beams at me before turning his attention to the menu cards which the hospitality manager has dropped on our table as he makes his way through the carriage. "I think I might try the tomato and basil soup followed by the succulent roast chicken."

CHAPTER THREE

We eat our lunch in near silence. Naturally, I do pay for it, though I find the cottage pie less than appetising. Still, I get through most of my meal then make my excuses and return to burying myself in my work. No way am I re-opening that bizarre discussion on spanking.

By the time we reach Newcastle, well over halfway to Edinburgh, I can bear the quiet no longer. And I am genuinely curious about these two men who were, briefly, my best friends once.

"Are you on your way home?" I ask Fraze. "To Hathersmuir?" I recall the name of his family estate located somewhere in the Scottish Highlands, though of course I have never been there.

He shakes his head. "I don't get home that often. We're both headed to a family wedding in Edinburgh. Another of my countless cousins…"

"Oh, I see. So you live in Peterborough?"

"No, Hatfield. It's good for commuting to the City." He nods across at Declan. "He plays for Peterborough these days, so it made sense to meet there and travel up together."

"I see."

Commuting? That suggests a job in London. Somehow, I always envisaged Fraze as some sort of *Monarch of the Glen* character, striding across heather-carpeted moorland, his clan tartan flapping around his knees. The smartly casual man seated opposite does not fit that image. "What do you do in the City?"

"Banking, along with one or two non-executive directorships."

"Do you miss the Highlands?" I wonder.

He shrugs. "Not especially. I manage a couple of trips a year back to Hathersmuir, but mainly the estate is run by my sister these days. You remember Miranda? She was at St Hugh's, too."

"Yes, though she was older than us, so I didn't really know her. You're a banker? I suppose that means you did eventually manage to pass a maths exam."

He grins, the expression lighting up his already too-handsome face. "Ellie, your faith in my profession is touching. I wouldn't put money on many of my colleagues passing a maths GCSE, if I'm honest. I confess I remain crap at algebra and geometry, but I never had any trouble understanding a column of figures or a balance sheet."

"Oh." I'm not certain how to respond to that, though I make a mental note to remember this conversation next time I need to speak to my bank about extending my overdraft. I turn my attention to Declan. "You used to play abroad, yes?"

He nods. "Barcelona."

"Then why…?"

His grin is wry. "I'm just thirty, and so far no serious injuries. That amounts to something of a charmed life, and my luck would eventually run out if I carried on playing in the top flight among all those hungry and ruthless youngsters. Premier League soccer is fucking brutal, and I've done my share of it. Add to that, I've nothing to prove. I was in the side that won the Champions League—twice—and the European Super Cup. I've been capped for Scotland over twenty times. There's plenty of other stuff I want to do with my life, so it made sense to transfer back home and settle down. I still play, I enjoy my football, but these days if I want to chill out in Edinburgh for the weekend, I can."

"What other stuff?"

"Media opportunities and business interests. I own a whisky distillery which does okay, but I want to spend more time on that and perhaps expand it. Most people would see peddling alcohol as not really compatible with a career as a sporting idol, so I guess I had to make a choice."

Fraze gives a snort. "Lyons whisky isn't alcohol. It's nectar."

Declan regards him under his dark eyebrows. "You would say that, but the distillery was started by your great-uncle, so you're biased."

"Doesn't make me wrong, though."

I'm struggling to keep up. "You mean you bought one of Fraze's family businesses?"

Declan shakes his head. "No. I inherited it. For some reason the old duke left Lyons Whisky to me when he died. At first I didn't take much interest, he left a lot of small bequests, but when the profits started to arrive in my bank account four times a year I began to take notice. I like to think of it as my pension fund."

"I never imagined you as a businessman."

"Oh. What did you imagine, then?"

"Well, sports, obviously. And I followed your career more or less. You tended to be in the limelight. I could see you as one of those football commentators on the television."

He shakes his head. "Not for me. Once I stop playing I'll be done with football. Time to move on. Lyons Whisky first, then I'll see what interests me next."

"You must have some ideas," I prompt.

"You mean besides spanking my old school friends?"

The flush starts somewhere near my navel and rises slowly but surely up my neck to engulf my face. I turn to stare out the window at the breathtaking Northumberland coastline as it hurtles past. I start at the touch of his hand on my shoulder.

"Turn around, Ellie."

I shake my head.

"Please."

I do as he asks, though with great reluctance. I don't know why this conversation embarrasses me as much as it does, but I'm finding it nothing short of excruciating. I have only to tell them to drop it, and I know they will, but instead I cringe and try to hide my mortification.

"I'm sorry. I've upset you…" Declan sweeps my hair from my face to reveal my still-flushed cheeks.

"No, it's just…"

"No more talk of spankings," Fraze announces.

At the same time he produces a small, cream-coloured business card from his inside pocket and slides it across the table to rest beside my laptop. "We do want to keep in touch, though. It's been too long. My address in Hatfield is on there, and on the back is my flat in Edinburgh. That's where we'll be for the next few days. He produces a pen and scrawls his mobile number onto the card, too. "There. No excuses."

"I don't have a business card, but this is my mobile." Declan scribbles his number onto the corner of one of my sheets of notes. "Call me. Now."

I do, and he quickly saves my number into his speed dial. "Right. So, where are you staying in Edinburgh, how long for, and do you have plans for this evening?"

*****

My plans for the evening amount to checking into my city centre hotel, eating dinner alone in the hotel restaurant, taking a long soak, and hopefully getting a decent night's sleep before my presentation tomorrow. I explain that to Fraze and Declan and manage not to succumb to their invitation to join them for a meal later.

It's not that I don't trust them. Rather, I don't trust myself.

At last the train glides to a stop in Edinburgh Waverley station. We all shuffle out into the aisle and start reaching for coats, luggage, briefcases. Declan hauls my ridiculous case from the shelf above our heads and sets it down in front of me as he reaches for his own orange holdall. It seems Fraze has travelled light, though I suppose as he's going to be staying at his own flat in Edinburgh he probably doesn't need that much.

I start down the central aisle, heading for the exit.

"Hold on." Fraze reaches for the handle of my case. "We'll see you into a taxi with that."

I start to protest that I don't need a taxi. My hotel is literally a two-minute stroll from the station. I soon abandon that when I realise they fully intend to see me to my hotel and will lug my case all the way if need be. A taxi suddenly seems much more reasonable.

They escort me from the train, then flank me as we walk up the slope leading to the main road outside where the taxis wait three deep. Declan hails one and Fraze hands me in, followed by my case.

"Which hotel?" he asks.

"Oh, The Scotsman. Really, I can manage…"

"Be sure to help her with that case," Declan instructs the cabbie as he hands the man a twenty-pound note. He leans in and kisses me on the cheek. "Call us. Please."

"I will," I promise, though what on earth I would have to say I cannot quite fathom.

"Hope it goes well tomorrow." Fraze also kisses me. "Good luck."

I clutch my laptop case on my knee as they close the door and step back from the vehicle.

A couple of minutes later, my cab pulls up at the front entrance of The Scotsman hotel, on the North Bridge, right in the heart of the city. My conference is taking place at the university, and I could have arranged for accommodation closer to the campus, but I love city centres and Edinburgh is one of the most elegant and intriguing. I'd already arranged for a two-night stay so that I could spend the day after the Symposium wandering around the rabbit warren of alleyways leading off the Royal Mile. I might even find time for a spot of shopping in the New Town, though the prospect of taking even more luggage back with me is enough to make me pause.

I check in and tow my case into the lift, then along the carpeted corridor to my room on the fourth floor. Normally I would unpack, even for a short stay such as this, but I can summon no enthusiasm for my usual neat and efficient ways. Instead, I abandon my case just inside the door and fling myself on the double bed to stare up at the ceiling. The room boasts satellite TV, WiFi, and a well-stocked minibar, but I ignore all these amenities as one word continues to swirl around in my head.

Spanking.

Add to that bare bottom, just to inject a spot of diversity, and I further cloud my thinking by pouring on hefty doses of embarrassment at my obsessive fascination with the ridiculous tableau it conjures up.

My imagination is working overtime.

Shame and humiliation are in there, too, because no matter how strenuously I denied it when Declan pointed it out, I see no merit in lying to myself. I am aroused by the idea, and curious, and itching to experience the wicked, forbidden naughtiness of it. The spanking would hurt, but that's only part of it. A small part. It's more the…the vulnerability. I imagine being exposed and defenceless, at the mercy of not just one man, but two.

And what a duo. Fraze and Declan were mouth-watering at school, but as adult men they are beyond gorgeous. At twelve I was too young to properly appreciate their rare masculine beauty, though I was certainly not oblivious to it, even then. Now, I am quite overwhelmed by them. Their scandalous suggestion, and my utterly inappropriate response to it make a heady cocktail, and not one likely to lay the foundation for a stellar performance in front of some of the finest clinical researchers in the northern hemisphere.

I need to get a grip. Fast.

As a scientist, I regularly come across anomalous data, the measurement which just doesn't fit, the seemingly incongruous finding nestled there among the predictable and the mundane. And in my experience, it is the unexpected, the unexplained, that usually holds the key to understanding. It is these ripples which cause us to expand our thinking, widen out theories to encompass more and more, to analyse, explain, and ultimately master.

This spanking phenomenon is no different. I need to know more. I need to research, I need to learn, to understand. I rarely have the time nor, indeed, the inclination to read fiction, but I'm not completely unaware of what's out there. If I was into leisure reading, my genre of choice would without doubt be erotic romance. Spurred on, and purposeful suddenly, I roll from the bed and pull my laptop from my briefcase. Moments later it's set up on the dressing table and I'm scrolling through lists of deliciously suggestive titles on Amazon. Tempting though they may be, I'm not in need of a Daddy nor do I want to know what it would be like to be taken by a barbarian warlord in this world or any other. Fraze and Declan are full of surprises, but I doubt shape-shifting is part of their charm, so I skip past the wolves, bears, dragons, and decide to narrow my search somewhat. I type 'spanking' into the search box and I sit back.

Bingo!

Domestic discipline and BDSM. Now those are the keywords I need. I buy an anthology of short stories which promises me stern Doms and feisty submissives, though I recognise neither myself nor Declan and Fraze in those descriptions. I just fancy the book, I suppose.

Trying another tactic, I type my keywords into Google images, and my screen is suddenly awash with pictures ranging from the ridiculous to the seriously disturbing. Too wide. I narrow my search, homing in on images which seem to me to be erotic and pleasing. My pussy quivers at the sight of reddened, clenching bottoms, occasionally soft flesh criss-crossed with vivid red stripes from a cane or strap.

Ouch! But still…

I find blogs and websites dedicated to the exquisite art of BDSM. I read of safe, sane, consensual play, of safe words and aftercare, of responsibility and trust.

And somewhere, somewhere deep inside, it starts to make sense. Not a lot of sense but some. Enough.

I'm not mad or perverted. Neither are they. Apparently Fraze and Declan like to get their kicks this way. Nothing wrong with that as long as everyone concerned is happy with the arrangement. And surprise, surprise, it seems I just might be wired that way, too.

I need to think, and the best place for that is in the bath, I find. I soak for the best part of an hour, luxuriating in warm, foaming bubbles scented with essence of apricots and pomegranate, then I use the shower attachment to rinse and wash my hair. I call down to room service while I'm drying my shoulder-length bob and ask for a baby spinach and ricotta ravioli with a side salad and a pot of tea. My food arrives whilst I'm getting dressed. I'm not wearing anything too showy, just a pair of smart grey trousers and a red blouse. I thank the waiter and tip him five pounds, then take the time to sit at the small table in an alcove close to my window overlooking the North Bridge and savour the delicate flavours. After all, having arrived at a decision, I'm in no hurry now. I have all night.

I check the hand-written address on the card Fraze gave to me. I don't know the street, but a quick squint at Google maps confirms what I suspected. The apartment is in the city centre, in the area known as New Town, perhaps a ten-minute walk from my hotel.

Should I phone first? They might have gone out. Or there may be someone else there with them. It's a family wedding, after all.

I decide against phoning. What will be, will be. I shrug into the smart grey jacket I bought for the conference and I let myself out of the room.

Edinburgh is a lively place by day and barely less so after dark. I'm surrounded by restaurants, bars, hotels, and tourist shops which remain open well into the night. Everywhere is light and sound. Music plays in the bars, the din of voices wrapped around more languages than I can recognise. Traffic continues unabated, horns sounding and doors slamming as fleets of taxis ferry people around. I enjoy the evening walk, pause to admire the floodlit splendour of Edinburgh Castle, the medieval fortress, which has dominated this city for the last nine centuries or so, and make a detour through the ornamental gardens running the length of Princes Street in the shadow of the castle. I exit and cross the busy shopping thoroughfare, then make my way through the geometrically arranged streets of elegant Georgian townhouses, built in the late eighteenth and early nineteenth centuries to offer gracious accommodation to Edinburgh's richest and most important citizens.

It suits Fraze and Declan nicely.

I find the correct street and halt before the neo-classical portal. A flight of eight regal steps lead up to the door which is painted a glossy black. Originally a single house for a wealthy merchant, the building has been divided into apartments. Four doorbells indicate my choices. I examine them and select the one marked Frazer-Lyons. I press it and I wait.

"First floor. Come on up."

The disembodied voice from the small grille beside the doorbells is followed by a sudden, sharp buzzing sound. I push the door, and it opens easily to my touch. I slip into the elegant entrance hall to be confronted by an ornate staircase right ahead of me and a less grand-looking pair of sliding metal doors to my right. The voice said first floor, right? I ignore the elevator and head for the stairs.

There is only one apartment on this landing. The door is graced by a single number one and the name Frazer-Lyons beside it in understated grey lettering. And it is ajar.

Did they see me, perhaps, walking along the street? Certainly, they seem to be expecting me. Or maybe I'm just that transparent. Well, I'm here now. I knock on the open door then step inside the apartment.

"Kitchen's on the right. Just leave it on the table. If you can hang on for a moment I'll—

Oh. It's you."

Fraze emerges from a door along the hallway and pauses to regard me. His surprised expression soon gives way to a lazy smile, enough to melt my knickers.

"You were expecting someone else." I state the obvious.

"Pizza delivery. Have you eaten?"

I nod. "Yes. At my hotel. I… I could come back later."

"You could, but I'm willing to bet you won't. I think we'd better hang on to you while we can." He turns as Declan appears in the doorway behind him. "We have a visitor."

"So I see. And a lot more appetising than a quattro stagione." Declan beams at me. "Hi, Ellie. Nice to see you."

"Er, right," I begin. "This was a mistake. I'm sorry, I just—"

"To what do we owe this pleasure? Was there something you wanted, Ellie?" Fraze's tone is soft, his eyebrow raised in that quizzical way he has.

Caught, I stand, rooted in the hallway and tell myself I should just be honest. I did come here looking for something, something tempting which they dangled before me and I turned down. I have to assume their offer still stands.

"I've been thinking…" My voice trails away.

There is silence for several seconds, until Fraze breaks it.

"Okay. What have you been thinking, Ellie?" Fraze's expression is more intent now, his tone sterner. He expects an answer.

"I was just… I mean, I wondered…"

"Yes? What can we do for you, Ellie?" Declan speaks to me in a softer tone, but I'm not fooled. He, too, expects an honest response.

"Spank me," I whisper. "Please."

CHAPTER FOUR

Both men smile, sexy grins that are enough to turn my insides to liquid. I swallow. Hard.

Declan takes a pace towards me. "I confess this is a surprise. We thought you might come around to our way of thinking, but not quite so soon."

"You…you talked about me?" I squeak.

"We talked about little else since you hopped into that taxi, to be honest," confesses Fraze. "Won't you come inside and we can discuss your…" He hesitates, considering. "…your requirements."

I make a show of consulting my watch. "I don't have that long, actually. I need to be up early tomorrow, for the conference…"

"A decent spanking can't be rushed. Shall we—?" Fraze is interrupted by the trilling of the doorbell. "Ah, now this probably is our supper. Dec, could you make Ellie comfortable while I see to this?"

Declan ushers me along the hallway, somehow relieving me of my jacket as we go, and guides me into the first room on the left. It's a spacious lounge complete with leather sofas and a television which takes up half a wall.

"We like to watch sport," Declan offers by way of explanation as I stand gaping at the monstrous screen.

I suppose they would, a professional footballer and an earl who used to play rugby for Scotland's amateur side.

"Please, sit down. Can I get you anything? A drink?"

I decline the drink but plop onto the expanse of dark brown leather nearest to me. Will they do it here? In this room? Will I have to bend over the arm of one of these sofas?

"Don't look so scared, Ellie." Declan sits next to me and loops an arm over my shoulders. "Nothing will happen unless you agree. You can back out any time."

Maybe he's right, in theory. In practice, if I turn and run now I might never have this chance again. And it is a chance, I see that now. My curiosity is on overdrive. I'm fascinated and terrified at the same time, but if I let this opportunity slip by I'll never forgive myself. I came here for a spanking, and I won't be leaving until I've had what I came for. The matter of the maths exam is important, to me at least, but that's a smokescreen really and only part of what motivates me. I have other reasons, too, reasons I'm only just beginning to acknowledge and explore.

"Here, drink this." Declan has ignored my words and poured me a glass of iced water. I'm on my second, very welcome sip when Fraze saunters through the door.

"I left the food in the kitchen. We can eat later."

"I'm sorry," I begin again, "for disturbing you."

He just grins and takes a seat opposite. I'm reminded of earlier, on the train, but this time there's no table between us. And no other passengers to worry about. Now, it's just the three of us and the elephant in the room which is my imminent spanking.

"Look at me, Ellie." Fraze's tone is quiet but compelling. I have no choice but to obey him. He continues, holding my gaze as he speaks. "We shouldn't rush this. We won't. But if you're nervous about it—and Ellie, we can both see that you are—the sooner we get it over with the better. The first time is always a big deal. Your second time will be easier."

"S-second time…?"

"Well, assuming you like it, obviously," says Declan. "But I think you will."

I swallow again and try to assemble some coherent thoughts. There are questions I need to ask. "Will it…? I mean… I get it, about the spanking and that it has to be on my bare bottom and all that. It's personal, very intimate…"

"Part of the unique charm of a spanking, I always think," offers Fraze.

I nod. Baring my backside for them is part of the thrill, I'm honest enough to admit that, if only for my own benefit. I reckon they already know.

"Go on," Fraze encourages me. He is leaning forward, his elbows on his thighs and his fingers intertwined in front of him.

I have his undivided attention. Beside me, Declan is equally intent.

"It's just…there are two of you. And earlier, you said something about sharing. About taking turns."

"Yes," agreed Declan, "we did."

"Would one of you watch while the other…?" I grind to a halt, hopelessly out of my depth. I have two degrees and a PhD in clinical research methodology and don't even know what questions to ask about a simple little spanking.

Declan squeezes my shoulders. "We could do it that way. Or we could both spank you at the same time. That would be our preference."

"Okay," I agree. I'm so far out of my comfort zone it hardly matters. "And would it…? I mean, what about sex?"

"What about sex?" Fraze tilts his chin, the glint in his emerald-coloured eyes softening perhaps a fraction.

"Would you expect me to sleep with you? With either of you? Both of you?" There. I've said it.

"Expect? No." Fraze shakes his head. "If you only want the spanking, then it stops there."

"Are you sure? What about what you want? Both of you?"

Declan is the one who answers. "Yes, we're sure. It's what you want that matters, Ellie. We've done this plenty of times before. We know how it goes, and you can believe us when we tell you that the fucking is an optional extra."

"You spank a lot of women?" I shouldn't feel jealous, but I do.

"Enough," admits Declan

"Together? Both of you at the same time?"

"Yes, quite often at the same time. It adds to the fun, we find."

"And…you fuck them, too?" I whisper.

"Yes, if they're up for it. And before you ask, we like to do that together, too."

Oh, dear sweet Lord. I should be running screaming from the building but instead I sit there, gazing into Fraze's mossy eyes while Declan caresses my clavicle and moisture pools in my knickers.

"I think… I mean, perhaps… I'm not sure if…" I have quite lost the power of speech.

Fraze grins at Declan. "Just the spanking for now, I reckon."

"Sounds like it," the other man agrees. "Shall we pick our implements?"

"Sure. I'll get my bag." Fraze stands and strides from the room.

Declan tops up my water glass as we wait. I'm glad of the cooling drink as my mouth has turned to sandpaper. A few moments later, Fraze joins us again and dumps a large holdall on the floor at my feet.

"My bag of tricks. I daresay we'll find something in here to suit you." He unzips the bag and opens it to reveal a collection of items I have only ever read about. I recognise a few paddles, canes, riding crops, and a whip. There are other things, too, but the sight of the whip unnerves me.

"No." I shake my head, start to get up. "This isn't what I thought…"

"Relax." Declan's hand on my elbow stops my rush for the door. "Baby steps. We're not going to get into anything too heavy, we promise. Look again, find something you do like."

"What…? I mean, I don't know…"

"What about this?" Fraze pulls a leather implement from the bag, a bit like a whip but with soft suede fronds dangling from the handle. "This is a flogger. It's very gentle, more sensuous than stingy." He holds it out to me.

I take the flogger in my hand and feel the softness of the leather. It's light, sort of floaty. "You could use this to spank me with?"

"Would you like that, Ellie?"

I nod. I would. I really think I would.

Declan rummages in the bag and comes up with one of the riding crops. "This has a bit more bite to it, but it's still gentle enough for a beginner." He flicks it against his hand. "Yes, I think this will be just fine."

Fraze shoves the bag out of the way and takes the flogger back from me. "So, shall we begin?"

"How many times… I mean, for how long…?"

"Until you tell us to stop. How does that sound?"

I flatten my lips. Fraze's response was softly spoken but with an edge of steel. I think I'm in good hands.

"What do I need to do? Do I undress?"

"You can. Or you could just drop your trousers to your knees, pull down your underwear, and lean across the back of the couch. We'll do the rest."

I close my eyes, take a deep, steadying breath. This is it. It's happening. Now.

I stand up and kick off my shoes, take another breath. Then another. Then, I reach for the button at the front of my trousers.

I'm glad the trousers are loose fitting because they slither down to my knees without any effort on my part. I look from Fraze to Declan and back again, seeking guidance.

"Kneel on the settee facing the back." Declan assists me in getting onto the sofa. "Now lean forward and rest your elbows on the top." He helps me to get into position. "Yes, that's good. Lift your bottom up a bit more and your shoulders need to be lower. Can we just lift this up a bit…?" He takes the loose hem of my blouse which had been neatly tucked inside my trousers and is now flapping loose about my hips. He rolls the fabric up my back to just above my waist to keep it out of the way. "Perfect. So now, we just need to slide these down…"

His fingers are on the waistband of my best satin briefs. He waits until I nod my permission, then he peels them down to my knees as well.

I am exposed, my bottom bared for spanking. They have only to tilt their heads a fraction and they will see my disgracefully wet pussy lips, my swollen labia, the pinkness of my slit. If I shift just a little, spread my legs the tiniest bit, they would see my clit, too, and then they would be in no doubt about how hopelessly aroused I am by all of this.

The room is warm, but the draught of air wafting across my naked buttocks reminds me of my vulnerability. A shiver ripples through my body, and when they both take up positions behind me, it's all I can do to remain in place.

"Such a lovely arse," observes Declan, "so pale and creamy."

"And curvy," adds Fraze.

Is he saying I have a fat bottom? I clench my buttocks, beyond humiliated.

"Perfect," Fraze clarifies, "fucking perfect."

"Are you ready, Ellie?" Declan lays his warm palm on my left bottom cheek and squeezes gently. I nod, so he continues. "Fraze will start, with the flogger. When you're warmed up a bit I'll join in, with the crop. We'll check with you often that you're all right, but you just have to say 'stop' and it's over. Do you understand?"

"Yes," I mutter. Now that I'm here I just want to get started. My imagination is all over the place. I need the reality of the spanking to ground me again. I need to know.

"Oh!" I let out a startled cry at the first feather-like stroke of the flogger. I'd clenched up, braced myself expecting something sharp, fierce. Instead I receive a soft whisper which dances across my backside, almost a caress. I glance back over my right shoulder, catch Fraze's eye.

"So far so good?" He raises that expressive eyebrow again and waits for my answer.

"Yes. So far so good."

I remain in place and sigh with each new stroke. I soon lose count. Fraze treats my buttocks and the backs of my thighs to the delicate shimmer of the flogger tendrils. They snake across my skin. Slowly, almost imperceptibly, the intensity builds. I'm not sure if Fraze is adding weight to the strokes or if it's just that my skin is more sensitive, but it starts to hurt. A little, but in a curiously good way. I writhe and shift as the heat builds and I lift up my bottom as though seeking more—I crave the sharpness of the strands colliding with my skin. I want him to hit me harder, faster. I let out a frustrated mewl when he pauses.

"My turn now." Declan lays his hand on my bottom again, and this time I flinch. He chuckles. "Nicely warmed up. Now for the sizzle."

He drops the first stroke onto my tender flesh, and I shriek. "Ow! That bloody hurt."

"It's a spanking, sweetheart. It's meant to hurt."

I screw up my eyes tight. I knew that, of course I knew. But the flogger was so gentle, so soft and...

"Aagh!" The second swipe with the crop really hurts, and without thinking I stretch my hand back to rub my abused bottom.

Declan catches my wrist before I can reach my smarting buttock. "No touching, Ellie. Hands in front."

His voice is firm, authoritative, and something flips over deep in my stomach. My pussy convulses. I was already wet but I'm dripping now and it's all I can do not to apologise.

Fraze moves around to the back of the sofa and crouches so his eyes are on a level with mine. "It's dangerous for you to reach back. Dec might hit your fingers and that could hurt you. Give me your hands."

He takes my hands and enfolds them within his own. His grip is firm, though not tight, but I know he would hold on to me if I were to slip up again. I find his presence comforting and manage a smile. I know it gets harder from now on.

Fraze nods over my shoulder at Dec, and moments later the third stroke sends a streak of fire across my bottom. I let out a scream and half expect Fraze to tell Declan to stop. He doesn't, but when I open my eyes again he is watching me, studying me. He dips his chin in that brief nod again, and Declan delivers the next stroke.

I manage to count six strokes with the crop before I know I've had enough. Almost. Perhaps just one more. I gnaw on my lower lip and curl my fingers around Fraze's. I'm the one gripping him now.

"Ellie?" Fraze's voice is gentle and somehow cuts through the throbbing waves of fiery pain. I meet his gaze. "Enough yet?"

I wait for a few moments, allow the sensations to ebb a little, catch my breath, then I shake my head. "Just a little more. Please."

Fraze glances over at Declan, and that silent communication thing goes on again. I get it. At last I get it. Declan is doing the business, and Fraze is looking out for me, making sure I'm coping. Between them, they're giving me what I need and more, and keeping me safe.

Declan brings the crop down again, this time across the fleshiest part of both my buttocks at once. My breath leaves me in a whoosh, and I gasp for precious oxygen.

"Are you ready to stop?" This time it's Declan who asks me.

I'm at my limit, I know that. So I should stretch my boundaries and manage one more, shouldn't I? That's the way to learn, to extend myself. It was always my way. "One more," I manage to croak. "Just one more."

Declan had been leaning over me but he straightens, swipes the crop through the air just once to create an ominous whistle, then he delivers the final stroke across the backs of my thighs.

I scream and lurch forward, into Fraze's arms. He holds me for a few moments, then stands up and helps me to turn around and lie on my side on the couch. I'm in time to watch Declan toss the crop into Fraze's bag of tricks, then he comes to sit beside my head. He lifts my upper torso from the leather cushion and rearranges me so I am using his thighs as a pillow. He combs his fingers through my hair.

"Didn't this used to be lighter? I seem to remember it was a dark-blonde colour."

"Mousy," I correct. "I had it dyed."

"It's nice. I like the red."

Fraze takes up his seat at the other end of the sofa and pulls my feet into his lap. I twist my neck to look at him, but he is unashamedly perusing my bottom.

"It feels swollen," I say. "And very sore."

Fraze grins. "I have some cream for that."

"No, thank you," I mutter. "I can manage."

"So…" Declan sweeps my hair back from my face with his fingers. "What's the verdict? How did you like your first spanking?"

I have to think about that. I need to process the sensations and confused reactions a bit more. I'm struggling to find the right vocabulary to describe my response. "It was nice," I manage, already knowing how inadequate that is, "but not what I expected."

"What did you expect?" asks Fraze.

"Well, I expected you to use your hands for a start."

"That would have been good, too," agreed Fraze. "Maybe next time."

"Next time?" I squeak, but I already know I'm going to want to do this again. The genie is well and truly out of the bottle now, my inner submissive has seen the light of day, and she won't be going back into the dark. "With you two again? I mean, would you want to? Even though we didn't... I mean, I wouldn't agree to sleep with you?" I hesitate. "I did like it. Really, I did, but I don't think I want to be spanked by anyone else."

Declan reaches to pat my hip, the light touch enough to make me wince. "Like we said, the fucking's optional."

Fraze nods his agreement. "And now we've found you again we intend to keep in touch, at least, so more fuck-free spankings could definitely be on the cards. Do you live in London?"

"Yes. Richmond. I work at the Imperial College, in the School of Medicine."

"I'm guessing Edinburgh's not a place you get to that often, then?"

"No, though it's a beautiful city."

"It is. My favourite. He reckons it's too cold and windy, though." Fraze tilts his head in Declan's direction. "He got soft, living in Barcelona."

Declan is unfazed. "Bloody Scots. They all think they're so hard. Any moment now he'll start waving his sporran and juggling with telegraph poles."

"You were born in Scotland, even if your mother did come from Ireland originally." Fraze grins at me. "For years I thought he was a leprechaun."

I forget my smarting, throbbing buttocks as they trade friendly insults. It's just like it used to be, when we were at school, apart from the fact that I'm naked from the waist down, obviously. I laugh, amazed at how comfortable I am with them.

"Don't we have a pizza waiting?" Declan starts to get up, and I shift to let him. "I'll get it."

I reach to pull up my knickers. "I've kept you from your food. You must be starving."

"No problem. Will you stay for something to eat?"

"I shouldn't, really. Tomorrow..."

"We'll walk you back after we've finished this." Declan dumps the pizza box on a low table and drags it in front of the sofa. He throws back the lid, and I'm hit by the delicious smells of the cheeses and tomato. Despite my ravioli and salad at the hotel earlier, my mouth is watering. I'm starving suddenly.

"Works up an appetite, doesn't it? A good spanking?" Declan hands me a paper plate.

I take it and stop arguing.

An hour later, the remains of the pizza lie congealing in the box, just a few bits of mushroom and a couple of crusts. We swilled the food down with bottles of Belgian lager, chatted about the old days and our adventures at St Hugh's, some of the crazier characters who were there. No mention was made of the maths exam. A clock somewhere chimes, reminding me of the time. It's eleven o'clock, I really do have a big day looming ahead of me, and I have to make an early start if I want to get out to the university campus in good time.

"I need to go."

"Okay." Fraze swings his long legs off the sofa and gets to his feet. He picks up the ruins of the pizza and ambles out of the room. When he comes back he is minus the pizza box and wearing his jacket. He flings a dark-blue fleece at Declan and hands me my grey jacket. "We'll walk you back to your hotel."

I know better than to protest, and in any case, a night-time stroll through Edinburgh with my two favourite men will be a pleasant and fitting way to finish a momentous day.

It takes us longer to get back to The Scotsman than it took me to walk to Fraze's apartment, but we're in no hurry. Fraze offers me his elbow, and Declan stations himself on my other side, so I link with him, too. The evening is cool but not uncomfortably so, and by now many of the tourist shops are closed. The restaurants and bars are still in full swing, though. Edinburgh by night is a lively place, and I'm utterly content to share the infectious ambiance with Fraze and Declan.

"When are you going back to London?" We're strolling along the North Bridge toward my hotel when Fraze pauses and asks me the question.

"I booked an extra night at the hotel, for tomorrow. I was planning on some shopping on Saturday and maybe get a train back on Saturday evening. My ticket's an open return, so I'm flexible."

"Don't go shopping. Come to Lucy's wedding."

"Lucy?" I frown up at him.

"His cousin, the one who's getting married," Declan clarifies. "The Honourable Lucinda Sinclair. She's marrying some guy she met on holiday in Italy, a Croation musician or something."

"Grgur Marak," says Fraze. "He's a cellist. He plays in an orchestra somewhere in Eastern Europe. I understand he's very good."

Declan gives a disgusted snort. "Well, at least no one could say she's marrying him for his money. Last I heard, Lucy's father owns four golf courses and more hotels than I can count."

Fraze shrugs. "But then, you never were that good at maths, as I believe Ellie may have pointed out. Old man Sinclair owns seven hotels, but I guess that would entail taking your other mitten off to count them all, so—"

"Stop it, both of you." I've heard enough. "I can't go to a society wedding. Apart from anything else, I haven't been invited."

Fraze isn't having that as an excuse. "You can be my plus one."

"No, she can be mine," insists Declan. "Why should you get the most beautiful woman on your arm?"

"I saw her first," Fraze counters. "On the train."

"Bollocks. Ellie, you can come with me."

"I can't. I don't have a dress for a do like that."

Fraze is incredulous. "What? You haul a suitcase weighing half a ton all the way from London, and you don't have even one posh gown in it?"

I shake my head. "No posh dress. Sorry."

"We'll send over a dress. It'll be here for you when you get back from your conference." He eyes me up and down. "Size twelve, right?"

"Well, yes, but I couldn't—"

"That's settled, then. Ah, here we are." Fraze halts at the steps up to my hotel. He grabs me in a close hug, then sets me away from him and leans in to kiss me. "You'll come with us? On Saturday?"

"I don't know…"

Declan whirls me around to face him. "Yes, you will. You know you want to."

He's right, I do. But I can't let them start buying me clothes.

"Send a dress, then. I'll be busy all day tomorrow, so I won't have time to go shopping. But I'll pay you back for it."

"Whatever." Declan traps my face between his hands and holds my head still while he brushes his lips over mine. "It's been good seeing you again, Ellie. Until Saturday, then."

He covers my mouth with his, and for a few seconds I lean in and simply enjoy the kiss.

"For fuck's sake, put the girl down. She has a speech to do in the morning. She needs to get some sleep."

Fraze has already opened the door leading into the hotel foyer. Declan releases me, and I sail past both of them as though I'm floating on air. I remember the practicalities just in time.

"Wait. I don't even know where this wedding is. What time…?"

"We'll pick you up at ten," says Fraze, "here, in the lobby."

CHAPTER FIVE

Fuck-free spanking. Is that what I want? Really?

It seemed safer, sort of sensible if that's the correct word to apply to last night's scenario, that I set that rule up front. Fraze and Declan agreed to it with no protest at all, though I'm certain it was not what they wanted. They put me first, gave me all that I asked for and no more.

I should be grateful but I find that I'm not. I feel sort of downcast and deflated this morning, just when I could do with being revved up and ready to sparkle at the Symposium. My libido, not usually a force to be reckoned with if I'm honest, has discovered a new lease of life and doesn't seem to be letting up any time soon.

I so need to get laid. Instead, I face a day of grinding, if scintillating scientific discourse. The reputation of my college and my professional standing are on the line. I have to perform.

I'm nervous about the conference, but that's healthy enough, born out of a natural desire to do well. I'm more worried about the wedding the following day. What if I don't know anyone there, which seems a pretty certain bet? Worse, what if I do know people and they remember me from school? I'll be going to the wedding with Fraze and Declan, but I can't expect them to babysit me the entire time. Who will I talk to? Will the other guests turn up their society noses at my Northern England accent, just like some of the snottier kids did at St Hugh's? My speech is a bit more refined now, years of working with academics from all over the world has sort of knocked the edges off, but I still sound like a lass from Leeds.

I give myself a mental shake. There's nothing wrong with Leeds, and there's nothing wrong with me. I may not have spent my weekends at the Pony Club and I definitely don't know one end of a croquet mallet from the other, but I'm bright, successful and respected in my field. I do interesting, important work. I make people's lives better. I should be able to hold my own in any company and I damned well will.

But hell, I'd so love to fuck Declan about now. Or Fraze. Or better still, both. Jesus, what have I become?

I set that question aside to be examined at another time. I have a presentation to deliver, a wedding to get my head around, and with any luck another bare-bottom trip over Fraze's sofa before too much longer. And if I have anything to say on the matter, fuck-free spanking will be off the menu next time.

I shouldn't be so surprised at my calm confidence as I commence my presentation, but I am. In fairness, I did my homework beforehand, assembled the right data, and when my name is announced and I get to my feet to appreciative applause from the assembled scientists and researchers, my peers and competitors, I'm ready to take on the world. I deliver my keynote speech, manage to switch slides at all the right points, pause at the more complex bits to allow my explanations to sink in, and reach my final slide unscathed. I'm feeling relaxed, confident and on top of everything as I scan the rows of faces, take a sip of water, and I invite questions.

There is discussion, naturally, but nothing I can't handle. My findings are pretty clear, not much room for dissent, though there's always someone ready to have a go. They don't get far, the data speaks for itself, and we scientists are suckers for hard evidence. An hour after I got to my feet I am shaking the hand of the conference chairwoman and bowing to the applause from the audience.

I nailed it!

The rest of the day is interesting, and having got my contribution to the proceedings out of the way first thing, I can relax and enjoy the workshops and presentations which follow. I'm no social butterfly, but a spot of professional networking doesn't go amiss, and there are plenty of delegates keen to congratulate me on my work.

It does my professional pride no harm at all, and by the time I find myself in the rear seat of a taxi on the way back to The Scotsman, I'm feeling pretty damn pleased with myself. I believe I might even enjoy myself tomorrow.

As I make my way up the front steps into the hotel lobby, I consider calling Fraze or Declan to find out if they're free this evening but decide against it. I'm horny as hell but exhausted, too. My libido will just have to wait.

"A parcel was delivered for you." The sleek receptionist bends to retrieve the large, bulky package from under the desk and places it on the counter in front of me. "I'll call a porter to help you carry it up to your room."

It's the dress Fraze and Declan insisted on sending over. I tip the porter, and as soon as my hotel room door closes behind him, I'm tearing the plain brown wrapping off to discover a large, square cardboard box from Harvey Nichols. Inside is a stunning concoction made of ice-grey, shimmering silk. It falls to just below the knee, and as I hold it in front of me and do a twirl, I can just see it will drape beautifully. It's exactly right, just what I would have chosen myself, though I might have gulped at the prospect of browsing round Harvey Nicks. I'm generally more of a Next chick myself, but a spot of indulgence doesn't go amiss occasionally, and I'm paid quite well. Not in Fraze's and Declan's leagues, obviously, but I can afford to treat myself when I want to. I rummage in the box for a price ticket or receipt but all I find is a pair of toning suede sandals with a dainty little heel, and a white silk clutch bag.

The dress is gorgeous. Thank you. How much do I owe you?

I send the text to Fraze and Declan simultaneously. Fraze responds.

Another spanking?

I'm equally quick to reply. *Seriously. It must have cost a fortune. I said I'd pay you back.*

Do you like it? This from Declan. *We thought the colour matches your eyes.*

When did Declan Stone become such a romantic?

I love it. Thank you. I can always go on their website and find out how much it cost. I mean it, I pay my own way.

Consider it a gift. For old times' sake.

But we agreed.

Please. Fraze ends his text with a small x.

I crumble.

Very well. This time. I hit Send, then follow up with another message. *Did you mean it, about a spanking?*

Yes, but could we start with dinner? What time can we pick you up?

I was going to have a bath, maybe watch a film.

Declan takes over. *What time, Ellie?*

Half past seven. I hit Send and wonder if I might get laid this evening after all.

The meal is delicious. Fraze has booked a table at a small trattoria just off the Royal Mile in Edinburgh's old town. They are keen to hear all about my presentation and share my elation that it went so well. Declan calls for a bottle of champagne to celebrate. For the next two hours we linger over aromatic tagliatelle, and once the champagne is gone we enjoy a crisp chianti, followed by cappuccinos and those little amoretti biscuits. It's after ten by the time we're finished.

"Would you like to come back to the apartment for a while?"

My hotel is closer, but I know what lies behind Declan's invitation and I'm most definitely up for extending our evening together.

"Yes, I would, actually."

We all stand, and Fraze helps me back into my jacket. Once we're out in the main road which runs through the old town, he lifts his hand to hail a passing taxi, but I grip his arm.

"No, let's walk."

We settle into a gentle stroll through the streets, me linking arms with both of them as I did yesterday evening. It's a cool evening but not unpleasantly so, and we exchange more anecdotes about St Hugh's as we make our way back to Fraze's apartment. Declan manages a fair imitation of old Mr Hennessy, the headmaster, then an even more hilarious rendition of Sister McHugh, the school nurse. By the time we arrive at the converted Georgian townhouse we're all in high spirits. Our mood sobers as we ascend the staircase to the first floor.

"Your choice, you do know that." Fraze takes my jacket and gestures me into the lounge again. "If you just fancy a nightcap…"

"I'd be back at The Scotsman raiding the minibar if that was all I fancied." I tilt my chin at the pair of them. "I... I brought condoms."

On my way back from the university, I'd detoured into the small pharmacy two doors up from my hotel. I am nothing if not prepared and ready to take responsibility for myself.

Declan grins at me. Fraze narrows his eyes, his nostrils flaring slightly. I wonder if perhaps he prefers to take the lead, though both my men seem decidedly on the dominant side. I wait for one of them to say something. Anything.

"Shall we take this into one of the bedrooms, then?" It's Declan who breaks the silence, glancing over at Fraze. "Yours is the biggest."

Fraze turns and marches from the room, stopping out in the hallway to beckon me with one aristocratic finger. "Come along, then, Ms Scott. And bring your condoms with you."

I follow Fraze along the corridor, Declan at my heels. Fraze leads us into the room at the end, and I pause just inside to take in the expensive luxury of the place. My own flat is nice enough but not in this class. The furnishings are dark wood, mahogany I'd say, and include a four-poster bed, two huge wardrobes, a dressing table, and a large writing desk. A gorgeous Queen Anne chair is set at an angle in front of the desk, as though he only just left it.

"Is that genuine?" I breathe, moving over to trail my fingers along the carved wood back.

"Of course. Eighteenth century. Its twin is in Dec's room."

"Ah, yes," I observe. "It would be part of a pair."

"You know about antiques?" Fraze lounges on the bed. "I'll give you a tour later, if you like."

"I'm no expert, but I do like old things. Especially beautiful things which are still in use."

"We like beautiful things, too. Come here, Ellie."

Fraze's tone has lowered an octave or three. Declan says nothing, but he is leaning on the pole at the foot of the bed, his arms crossed. Both men allow their gazes to travel over every inch of me and make no secret of their appraisal. I start to feel like a precious artefact myself.

"Come here," Fraze repeats. "Stand at the foot of the bed and keep still. I'll watch while Dec undresses you."

I swallow but obey. This is no time to be coy. I haven't yet fathomed how this will all work, exactly, but I know it's what I want. There are three of us in this relationship.

Declan steps forward, cups my chin in his hand, and kisses me. I part my lips and gasp as he plunges his tongue into my mouth, and lift my hands to grip his arms when he tilts my head back to deepen the kiss. My knees are ready to give way by the time he lifts his mouth from mine.

"So responsive. We're going to have lots of fun with you, little Ellie Scott." His voice is rich and dark, like chocolate. His words wash over me, through me, and my panties dampen.

Oh. My. God.

Slowly, deliberately, Declan circles me. He stops behind me and undoes the buttons at the back of my top. Then he tugs it from the waistband of my knee-length pencil skirt. He grasps the hem and raises it. Without being asked, I lift my arms to let him slide the garment off. He ignores my crimson bra for the time being, preferring to undo the button at my left hip and then slowly slide the zipper down to loosen my skirt. He peels the fabric down over my hips and my legs to let it fall in a heap around my ankles. I bless the impulse which took me into Ann Summers' a few weeks ago, where I purchased a gorgeous matching set of bra and panties in a siren shade of red, and the sleek pearl-coloured stockings. Now, standing before these two beautiful men wearing just those items of lingerie, I feel every bit as beautiful as Fraze suggested.

Declan is still positioned behind me. He kisses the nape of my neck, then unclasps my bra. The cups fall forward, free, and I briefly catch them in my arms before allowing the bra to drop to the floor, too. Fraze's lip quirks as he peruses my naked breasts, and I wait for him to say something.

His appreciative silence speaks far louder to me than words might have. His eyes darken, the green deepening to near black. My nipples swell and stiffen under his scrutiny, and I know Fraze will not have missed any of the detail of my response. I might have lifted my hands to cover myself, quite overwhelmed by the intensity of his gaze, but Declan's hand in the middle of my shoulder blades and his murmured command to lean forward breaks the spell.

I bend at the waist and place my hands on the mattress, on either side of Fraze's feet. I look up and meet his steady gaze as Declan peels my panties away. I step out of them when he taps my ankle.

"I like the stockings. They can stay," announces Declan, straightening.

When I would have stood upright again also, he places his hand on my back. "No. You stay there. Here's how this will work. You'll look at Fraze while I spank you. Don't look away, and don't move. You maintain eye contact with Fraze all through your spanking. Then, after, when I put my fingers inside you, you'll keep on looking at him. You'll probably come around about then, but still you maintain eye contact. Fraze will watch, he'll be there, inside your head while you lose control. He and I will be talking, but you'll say nothing unless one of us asks you a direct question. When I fuck you, you'll still be looking at Fraze. He'll be in your head while I'm in your pussy." He pauses, "Any questions?"

Yes! I have a million questions. But I shake my head. "No. I understand."

"One last thing. If you need us to stop, you can say so. I'm not going to hurt you—well, not really—but it will be intense and intimate. If it's too much, just say 'red' and we stop. Is all that clear as well?"

"Yes," I murmur. "Quite clear."

"In that case…"

I jerk forward when Declan lands the first swat on my upturned buttock.

"Look at me," demands Fraze, and I realise that I already allowed my eyelids to droop.

I lock my gaze with his and try to concentrate.

Declan is using his hand to spank me, and it hurts every bit as much as the crop he used yesterday. The sound of the slaps reverberates around the room, louder than I imagined. I count the spanks, and by the time he reaches ten my bottom feels to be on fire. I'm chewing on my lower lip, and fighting back tears when we reach a dozen, and let out my first yelp of pain at fourteen.

Fraze nods, the movement barely perceptible, but Declan must have seen it because he stops spanking and instead lays his hand on my smarting bottom and massages my buttocks in large, slow circles. I sigh—the relief is awesome.

"Better?" Fraze asks me the question after perhaps a minute of the soothing caress, his eyebrow raised as he awaits a reply. When I don't speak, he continues. "That was a direct question, Ellie."

"Yes," I say. "Better."

"She's ready. You can carry on." Fraze never breaks eye contact with me when he speaks to Declan.

The spanking starts again, and I'm certain that Declan has ramped it up. It hurts. Really, really hurts. Each swat causes me to cry out and come up on my toes. Neither man seems to mind my squeals and yelps, so I assume they don't count as talking. It never occurs to me to say 'red'. Instead, I clench my buttocks and try to absorb the pain whilst Declan continues his relentless onslaught on my poor bottom. The fire snakes over my tender skin with every resounding slap and wonder why I ever thought I wanted this.

Fraze's handsome but stern features waver and sway before me as I view them through the tears I am helpless to stem. They stream across my cheeks to drip from my chin.

"Are you wet, Ellie?"

Fraze's question catches me off guard. I am still managing to look at him but I can't find words to answer. I try to think, but no coherent response emerges.

"I'll check." Declan places one heavy palm on my throbbing bottom and draws the other slowly between my thighs, through my swollen folds. He swipes back and forth, rubbing my pussy lips and scraping my clit with his fingertips. "Hell, yes, she is. She's drooling down here."

"A pain slut, then?"

"Yeah, seems like it. Is that right, Ellie? Do you get off on being hurt?"

"I… I don't know. I…"

"Truth, Elllie." Declan continues to stroke my pussy lips and slides two long fingers right inside me. "This dripping pussy tells us what we want to know, but we'd like to hear it from you, too."

"Yes," I sob. "I like it when you hurt me. I want…oh! Oh, God…"

He drives his fingers in and out of my cunt, deep and fast, then adds a third. My entrance is stretching, but when Declan twists his hand to rub against some spot inside me, my knees are about to buckle.

I close my eyes when the orgasm boils and starts to erupt.

Declan's hand stills. I whimper my disappointment and frustration.

"Look at me, Ellie. If you want this to continue, then you fucking look at me." Fraze growls his command, and I get it. Declan stopped because I closed my eyes. There's to be no hiding from them, no privacy. If I want the orgasm, it will be on their terms.

"I'm sorry," I whisper, forcing my eyelids apart and meeting Fraze's emerald gaze again. He doesn't acknowledge me. His curt nod is the signal for Declan that I am complying and to start up again.

Declan's touch is deft, his fingers skilled. In moments, my climax surges forward again, threatening to overwhelm my senses. My body clenches and convulses, and it takes a supreme effort of will to keep my gaze locked on Fraze's. My pussy contracts around Declan's long, thick fingers while he uses his free hand to rub and squeeze my clit. Fraze's face shimmers before me, partly obscured by the white light which explodes somewhere in my head. I hear sounds, grunting, my own inarticulate muttering as my senses shatter.

And still I look at Fraze, my obedience as perfect as I can make it. My reward? The slight curl of his lips when Fraze smiles.

"She's a fast learner," he observes.

Declan's fingers slow, and he withdraws them. The tension leaves my body, and I would have flopped forward onto the bed had he not wrapped his arm around my waist from behind.

"Oh no you don't. I'm not finished with you yet."

I stiffen my arms and regain my balance, then lift my gaze to meet Fraze's once more.

"Good girl," he growls, at the same time reaching behind him to the bedside table. He pulls out the top drawer and grabs a condom, then tosses the foil packet to Declan.

I am only dimly aware of the snap of the foil. Moments later, Declan stretches his arm around me again, from behind, and lays the tip of his left middle finger on my clit. He circles the swollen nub, while with his right hand he lifts my knee up and out until it rests on the end of the bed and I am fully open to him.

"Eyes on Fraze," he murmurs, positioning his cock at my entrance. "Don't look away or I'll take my belt to you afterwards."

I gasp when he drives his cock deep inside me with one long, even stroke, filling me. I squeeze and clench, the crown of his erection nudging my cervix. He holds still and waits for me to stretch, to adjust. He withdraws, and I moan. He almost pulls right out of me, then thrusts deep again. I pant and let out the occasional groan in response to his steady fucking, slow at first, then faster, harder, he drills into my welcoming body, setting up a compelling rhythm.

"Fuck, she's tight. And hot." Declan's voice is a low growl. He angles his thrusts to hit that same spot he found with his fingers.

In moments I'm soaring again, my body quivering, reaching for my next climax. The walls of my pussy contract to grip him, demanding more friction, more intensity. I want it harder, faster, rougher, and that's what Declan delivers.

And all the while, all the time he is pounding his cock into my cunt, my eyes never leave Fraze's. He sears into my soul as I come again, witness to my most intimate moment, my response bared to him, naked, vulnerable.

Declan fucked me, it is his cock in my pussy, his semen in the condom, but Fraze had me, too.

When Declan pulls out, I do, at last, crumple onto the bed. I lie still, panting, but not for long. Fraze shifts to pick me up in his arms, then cradles me against his chest while Declan rights his clothes and disposes of the condom in the bin.

CHAPTER SIX

"I'll take her now." Declan, fully dressed again, comes to lie beside us. He never looked sexier.

My pussy clenches at the memory of his thick cock filling me. Fraze sits up and deposits me in Declan's arms.

"You have a choice here, Ellie." Fraze is the one who now cups my chin and grazes his lips over mine before tipping my face up so I have to meet his gaze. "If you've had enough, you can get dressed and we'll take you back to your hotel. Or you can stay here for the night, that's fine, too. We'll just let you sleep. But if you want to carry on, we have plenty more in store for you."

"More? More spanking? I don't think I want more of that, not quite yet."

Fraze grins. "No. One spanking is enough for now. What I have in mind is more kinky fucking."

"Oh." My pussy is still tingling, and I feel sort of well-used, though nicely so. Declan wasn't exactly gentle, not that I wanted him to be. I really should decline further fucking, kinky or otherwise, but the clenching deep inside me tells a different story. Perhaps I am a pain slut, or maybe just a slut full stop. But if there's more to be had, I won't be going back to The Scotsman any time soon.

"I think I'd like to stay. But not to sleep." I glance up at Declan. "Will you be the one staring at me this time?"

He shakes his head. "No. I'll be holding you still for Fraze, though. And there'll be no staring. In fact, you'll be blindfolded."

Open-mouthed, I take in what Declan just said.

Holding me still? Blindfolded? Holy shit!

"Are you still up for this, Ellie?" Fraze is still cupping my chin. "Same rules as before—no talking unless one of us asks you a direct question and if you want to stop, you just say 'red'."

I look from one to the other, then I slowly nod. "I'm up for it," I whisper. "Bring it on."

Fraze grins, kisses me again, then rolls from the bed. He goes over to the large, carved dressing table and extracts a midnight-blue tie from the top drawer. He tosses it to Declan. "That's for the blindfold. Will you need any more to use as restraints?"

"No, because Ellie's going to stay exactly where I put her, aren't you, sweetheart? I won't need to tie you up, will I?"

I suppose he won't, not if he says so.

"I... I'll keep still," I manage to croak.

"The blindfold first." Declan arranges the tie—pure silk if I'm any judge—over my eyes and ties it behind my head. "Can you see anything?"

"No," I confirm. My voice is quivering. I can hear it so I'm sure they can, too.

"Good. Now, you'll lie back and lean on me, your bottom between my legs and your shoulders against my chest."

He waits until I get in position. The soft cotton of his shirt grazes my naked skin seductively. Even the scrape of the duvet rubbing against my spanked bottom has a rough sensuality about it. I wriggle in his arms.

"Now, reach up and clasp your hands together behind your head."

I do as Declan tells me, conscious that the position lifts my breasts up, emphasising my tight, stiff nipples. As though he reads my mind, Declan cups my breasts and squeezes them together.

"Gorgeous tits, Ellie." His voice is soft, close to my ear.

I've always considered them to be a bit on the small side, but in this moment I'm ready to soak up any compliment that comes my way. I feel gorgeous, and sexy and so, so ready for this.

He takes the time to roll my pebbled nipples in his fingers, then releases my breasts to put his hands behind my knees. He lifts them, spreading my legs apart as he does so.

At once, I am exposed, open, completely available for whatever Fraze plans to do to me. As if to emphasise my vulnerability, Declan repeats his instructions.

"You're not to move or speak without permission. You can make other sounds if you have to. Understood?"

"Yes," I murmur. "I'm ready."

For a few moments there is just silence. I wait, anxiety and arousal warring within me, though arousal is winning. I run my tongue across my dry lips and resist the urge to ask what they mean to do to me.

A faint buzzing startles me. I jerk, and Declan's arms tighten around me.

"Relax," he breathes into my hair. "Trust us."

I do trust them. I really do. I manage a small nod and allow my muscles to loosen.

I have no need to ask why they blindfolded me. My imagination runs rampant, every sound, every whisper of movement is magnified. The musky scent of Declan's aftershave fills my nostrils, the heat of his fingers warms my skin as he holds my legs apart. I can hear Fraze's breathing, and the bed shifts beneath me when he sits between my spread thighs.

Fingertips, they must be Fraze's, leave a trail up my inner thigh, first the left, then the right. He stops before he reaches my pussy, but I feel his eyes on me as clearly as if he did touch me there. Then he runs his hands up both thighs at once, almost to the top. The buzzing is still there, but faint.

I lift my hips, desperate for him to touch me. I'm ready to plead, to beg if I have to. The suspense is awful. Awesome. Anticipation takes my breath away, but still he makes me wait. They make me wait.

Cool. The cool whisper of breath shimmers across my throbbing clit. A moment later Fraze wraps his lips around the swollen bud and he sucks.

I scream. The sensation is indescribable, sudden and unexpected despite my frenzied anticipation, and completely overwhelms me. It is erotic, achingly intimate, intense. It's too much. I strain to slam my legs closed, but Declan's grip is unshakable. I start to unclasp my hands as though I might use them to protect myself from the crashing waves of sensation.

"Don't," Declan growls in my ear, "don't move."

My orgasm barrels up out of nowhere. My pussy is clenching on emptiness, my juices dampening the duvet under me as I shake in Declan's arms. Fraze shifts his position and uses his tongue now to tap my clit, first one side, then the other. Then he laps at the tip before taking it between his lips again. This time his teeth scrape the sensitive knot of tissue, and I know I'll come in the next few moments. I abandon any attempt to stem the waves of pure sensation and allow my climax to carry me along.

Fraze continues to lick and suck my clit, drawing the orgasm out, wringing every last frisson of response from me. The pleasure seems endless, bottomless, though eventually I lie limp, draped across Declan's chest.

"So, that's taken the edge off for her. Now we can have some fun." Fraze's soft Scottish brogue sounds playful but is laced with a thread of something darker, more dangerous. His fingers replace his tongue, and he strokes my pussy idly. "New rules, Ellie. Are you listening?"

"Yes," I manage.

"That's the last orgasm you'll steal. In future, you ask before you come. Is that clear?"

"But, I couldn't help it. When you… you…"

"You need to learn to control yourself, Ellie. We can help you with that, by spanking you when you screw up. I think that would concentrate your mind a little. What do you think, Dec?"

"Worth trying," agrees Declan.

"Okay, so we continue." Fraze pauses, then sinks two fingers into my pussy.

I gasp, whether in surprise or pleasure I'm not certain.

"Does this hurt?" Fraze thrusts his fingers in and out, quite gently, but driving deep each time.

"No, no it feels…good."

"Such a slut," Fraze chuckles. "Would you like something else in here, something to make you feel even better?"

I nod, past caring. "Yes, please."

The buzzing is louder suddenly, and I realise what it is. A vibrator. Will it be big, a dildo, or small, the bullet sort?

Fraze parts my pussy lips with his fingers, and I jerk hard when he presses the toy against my spread labia. The sensation is acute—all my senses seem to sharpen to one point right at my core. He shifts the vibrator forward, closer to my clit, and I know without a shadow of a doubt that if he touches me there I'll come again, permission or no.

"Please…" I croak. "Please don't."

Fraze lifts the toy away from me. "Is that meant to be your safe word, Ellie?"

What? No! I shake my head wildly, confused. "I didn't mean that. I just… I'll come if you carry on, and I thought you said—"

"I did say. I also said you weren't to speak unless in answer to a question or to use your safe word. 'Please don't' is neither of those, but because you're new to all this I thought it best to check."

"I'm sorry. It was just…" I stop, gather my wits and think. At least now I know they will respect my safe word. "I'm learning. I won't speak again. I promise."

"Good girl." Declan murmurs the encouragement into my hair and kisses my elbow. "How about I help you out? Does this work to take your mind off what Fraze is up to?" He cups my breasts and kneads the lower curves, then takes my nipples between his fingers as he did before. "Here's a little trick. If you feel you might disgrace yourself again and come by accident, you can ask me for help, and I'll squeeze your nipples, like this." He demonstrates, and I yelp as the discomfort bites. "Or I can twist, too, just to make sure…" He gives me a demonstration, only releasing my tortured nubs when I squeal. "Do you think that would stop an orgasm for you?"

I nod. Right in its tracks.

"Okay. You can place your hands on my arms then. When you need me to help you out, just give a couple of sharp taps, like this." He taps my thigh, twice, firmly. "Can you do that, Ellie?"

"Yes," I reply. "Th-thank you." A thought occurs to me. "I have a question. Is it okay to ask…?"

"Go ahead." Declan is cradling my breasts now, stroking my throbbing nipples. It feels so good…

"Am I allowed to speak to ask permission to come?"

"I guess that's fair." This time it's Fraze's voice I hear. "Now, are we done with the chit chat?"

"Yes. I'm ready…"

Despite my assurance, I can't prevent the quivering when he again spreads my labia apart. Fraze is gentle, and my pussy is dripping wet, so when he inserts the buzzing toy it slips easily into place. It is small and slides into my slick channel to nestle there. Fraze must have altered the controls because the sensation changes. It becomes a strong pulse, sending rhythmic waves of pleasure right to my core. It is sensual, but calming, too, less intense than the direct vibrations against my clit. I can handle this, it feels nice, very, very nice…

"Oh!" I let out a surprised yelp when Fraze dips the end of his finger into my anus. I hadn't expected that.

He stills his finger, though the tip remains inside my rear hole. "Problem, Ellie?"

Is it a problem? My head is reeling, this is all moving so fast. Even so, I feel safe, somehow protected with Declan and Fraze. If it were anyone else it would be a problem, a huge no-no. I run my tongue over my lips and note that they are dry.

"N-no, not a problem, exactly. I just … I've never…"

"Okay, I get that. I won't hurt you, Ellie."

I flatten my lips and give a sharp nod.

Declan speaks from behind me. "Do you want a drink, sweetheart?"

I twist my neck as though I might look up at him, despite the blindfold. "Could I? Is that allowed?"

He chuckles. "Of course."

I hear a sharp snap, the sound of a bottle opening, then the plastic nudges my lips. Declan tips up the bottle and I swallow the cool water. Nothing was ever so delicious, or so welcome.

"Another new rule. You can ask for an orgasm, and you can ask for water."

I nod again and relax against him, the insistent pulsing from the vibrator caressing my inner walls. There's pleasure, but not the clamorous, demanding friction that would hurtle me toward another climax.

Fraze withdraws his finger, then pushes it into my anus again. He swirls it around, and my opening loosens. He inserts a second digit, and though it's tight I manage to accept it.

The feeling is odd, an invasion, intrusive, but deliciously wicked. He thrusts his fingers fully into me, and I feel impossibly full, stretched, and exquisitely used. If I was a cat I would purr. I might anyway.

The scrape of Fraze's thumb over my clit jolts me from my sensual languor. Sensation builds as he rubs the engorged nub slowly, then taps it hard.

"Please, I want to come. May I…?"

"No," growls Fraze.

"But I…" Another wave of orgasmic pleasure threatens to engulf me. In desperation, I tap Declan's arm, then immediately scream when he twists my right nipple in his fingers.

"Is that better, Ellie?" Declan murmurs in my ear, now rolling the abused nub gently.

I am shaking, my senses scrambled. Every touch, every stroke or caress is perilously sweet—enticing yet terrifying. They control my senses, not me. I understand that now. I experience the helpless vulnerability as pleasure spreads right out to my fingertips and I groan. They won't give me permission to come, but Fraze can and will force my orgasm from me whenever he chooses to. Declan can help, but at a price. If I come, when I come, I will be punished. Another spanking, or maybe something else?

And all the time I try to process this riot of conflicting responses, the toy buried deep within me continues to emit its inexorable pulsing.

"Please," I gasp, "I need to come. I can't…"

"Count to ten," commands Declan softly. "Hold on for a count of ten, then you can have what you need."

"Really?" I must sound pathetically needy.

"Really," agrees Fraze.

"Is this helping?" Declan squeezes both my nipples.

It hurts, but the pain is more muted now, less of a shock. It's enough to hold my attention, though.

"Yes, I think." I manage to grind out the words.

Fraze peels back the folds of flesh which would usually shield my clit, and I swear the swollen nub stands to attention for him. He takes it between his fingers, then laps at the tip with his tongue.

My hips jerk forward, I have no control over them, but the steady pressure of Declan's fingers pressing my nipples keeps me grounded. I count the pulsing waves inside my pussy since that seems easier than trying to think for myself. One. Two. Three…

When Fraze sucks my clit, I tap Declan's arm hard. Dutifully he increases the pressure, and this time I welcome it. The pain purifies me, fortifies me. It gives me focus.

Four. Five. Six.

Fraze somehow manages to increase the strength of the pulsing waves. They buffet me now, demanding my response. He finger-fucks my arse at the same time as he takes my clit in his teeth, makes his tongue hard and presses against the underside of the sensitive bud. It's too much, I can't…

Seven. Eight.

Just hang on. Almost done…almost…

Nine. Ten!

"Now," I sob. "Please, now…"

"Yes." Declan softens his grip and is again stroking my nipples. "You can come when you like."

My orgasm rips through me with the force of a tornado. I let out small, inarticulate moans of appreciation, sighs of pure delight. Shafts of white light fill my stolen vision, a kaleidoscope of fireworks erupt in my head. I swear the Earth moves under me. Then it fucking moves again and I'm floating.

As the crescendo of sensation recedes I am limp, washed out. I sag in Declan's arms when Fraze withdraws his fingers from my rear hole then slides the pulsing toy from my pussy. Declan removes the blindfold, and I blink in the light. He is no longer holding my legs apart, but I make no move to straighten or close them. I'm content to lie here, my thighs splayed, my pussy still drooling as my heartbeat slowly returns to normal.

"That was…amazing," I eventually manage.

"I thought so, too. Dec?"

"Yeah, fucking awesome. You want a condom?"

"Yes. Top drawer, on your right."

"You…you're going to fuck me?" I'd sort of assumed that we were done.

"I reckon you earned it," comments Fraze. "Unless you want to call a halt now. Your choice."

I guess this is the benefit of a threesome—I get their undivided attention, their combined efforts to both pleasure and hurt me, and double the fucking.

"I don't want to stop."

"Good," agreed Fraze. "I was hoping you wouldn't."

I watch, still slightly dazed from the erotic workout I've already had. Fraze unbuckles his belt, then unzips his trousers. Somehow, I had managed to forget that whilst I'm naked they are both fully dressed. Fraze's cock springs free, and I can't help but admire it. I never had the opportunity to actually see Declan's cock before he drove it into me, but it felt huge. I have a somewhat limited frame of reference, but Fraze, too, looks enormous. He unrolls the condom over it, the slightly darker, smooth head already dribbling pre-cum.

"I wanted to touch you."

"Next time, baby." Fraze smiles at me, then grabs my ankles and drags me towards him.

Declan shifts so he is lying across the bed, at right angles to me. He leans over, his lazy, sexy smile filling my vision.

"Next time Fraze fucks you, you'll be sucking my cock."

"Oh. But…" I gape at him and try to get my head around this latest twist.

"Not this time. We agreed on baby steps, sweetheart. But something to look forward to, yes?"

"Yes," I breathe, then I completely lose the thread of the conversation when Fraze sinks his cock balls-deep in my waiting pussy.

He delivers several short, sharp thrusts, and I grope for something to hang on to. I clamp my fist around Declan's wrist, then close my eyes to savour the build-up of friction. My inner walls convulse, gripping Fraze hard. I squeeze around him deliberately, amazed that I am able to tighten even more. Fraze groans, his eyes now closed, and his beautiful mouth twists in a grimace. He drives his cock deep, his thrusts hard and fast, pounding me.

Pleasure soars. I might even manage another climax. Perhaps…

Fraze shifts his position so he is kneeling and my hips are resting on his thighs. He looks down at me from hooded eyes, the emerald glint of dark lust pinning me to the bed. He glances up, beyond me.

"Dec, I need our girl to come."

"On it." Declan uses his free hand, the one I am not clutching in my fist, to reach over and flick my clit.

I let out a strangled moan, beyond aroused, beyond pleasured. Fraze is fucking me hard, and Declan's deft touch on my clit sends me soaring again. As Fraze fills me, as Declan strokes and rubs, my pussy convulses. The climax is on me before I can think to seek permission, if that were even needed now. My whole body shakes as I lose control again, as I surrender totally to my two lovers.

CHAPTER SEVEN

It's five minutes before ten. I perch on the edge of the sofa in the lobby of The Scotsman and wait for Fraze and Declan. My wedding outfit is in a small bag at my feet, and I am wearing casual jeans and a loose top. Just before the taxi dropped me off last night after my night of debauched and utterly delightful sex with them, they told me that the wedding is to take place in Pitlochry, a town north of Edinburgh, and that we'll have a drive of a couple of hours. They told me to dress for comfort and expect to change when we arrive. They also told me to check out of my hotel as I had planned to, and that I will be staying with them tonight. We will all travel back to London together tomorrow.

My bill is settled, my ridiculously heavy luggage propped up next to me. I can either stow my case in the boot of the car or leave it here at the hotel to collect before we catch our train. A draught of cool air wafts through the entrance as the door swings open. Declan strides across the plush carpeting. He, too, is dressed casually in black denim jeans and a plain grey T shirt. He beams at me.

"Nice and punctual, I see. This yours?" He leans in to kiss me on the mouth, then reaches for my suitcase.

"Yes, I didn't want to be late. There might be traffic…"

"We'll be fine. Formalities dealt with?" He cocks an eyebrow in the direction of the receptionist who is gawping at him. A football fan, no doubt.

"Yes," I confirm. "I could leave that here and—"

"It's fine. Shall we go, then? The car's on a double yellow line outside."

"Right." I grab my purse and the bag containing my beautiful grey silk dress and I follow him through the plate glass doors.

I don't know what I expected to find waiting for me at the foot of the steps, a nice car, obviously, but the sleek limousine with liveried driver standing beside the open rear door takes my breath away.

"Oh. Are we being driven?" Silly question, but out it comes.

Declan waves aside the driver when the man makes to take my case. He hauls my luggage around to the rear boot and pops it open. "We were planning to go up in Fraze's Audi, but this seemed better now there are three of us. More comfortable." He drops my case into the cavernous boot and closes the lid. "Hop in."

I scramble into the car's interior and I am at once conscious of the luxury. I'm met by buttery soft leather upholstery, a bank of controls for windows, air conditioning, sound system, even a minibar. And, of course, Fraze, lounging across one of the seats.

"Morning, gorgeous. Did you sleep well?" he drawls in that sexy cadence of his.

"Like a log." It's true. I was so exhausted when I got back to The Scotsman at around one in the morning that it was all I could do to get undressed before collapsing into my bed.

"That's good. So, you'll be fresh as a daisy now. Here, we got you this on the way round." Fraze waits until I sink into the seat opposite him, then hands me a disposable cup of coffee. He shows me how to flick out a small table to my left, and I perch the cup there.

"Thank you. I had breakfast, but this is very welcome."

Declan gets in behind me and sits at the other end of the seat. He stretches out his long legs, and Fraze hands him a coffee, too. "Thanks." He turns to me. "It's a long drive, but there's no hurry. The wedding isn't until two, so we can stop on the way if you like."

"I'm fine. Thank you, though."

Declan winks at me. "Yes, I think I'd have said you were fine, too."

The limousine purrs into life and glides away from the kerb. We're off.

We don't stop on the way but arrive in Pitlochry just after twelve so we have time for a leisurely lunch in a pub before making our way to the hotel, which is to be the scene for this social extravaganza. When we arrive, Fraze checks us in. He's booked a room for our use during the day, a place to change, to freshen up, to have a nap if need be. The ceremony is due to start in an hour or so, so we go up to our room to change into our finery.

I should be shy, perhaps, about stripping in front of them, but we are way past all that. I get the use of the bathroom first. I showered at my hotel, so now, clad in just my underwear, I apply some light makeup, brush my hair, then spray myself with my favourite Fendi perfume. Satisfied, I stroll back into the bedroom to find both my men in grey morning suit trousers and starched dress shirts. Their sleek, tailored jackets hang from the front of the wardrobe door, and their top hats are tumbled on the bed.

"Are you any good with cravats?" demands Declan, prodding at the crumpled mess around his neck.

"I can do a barrel knot if that helps."

"Shit, yes. Anything…"

I stand in front of him and smooth out the creased affair he has made of his cravat, then stand his collar up. I wrap the cravat around his neck with a longer length on the right, then make a loop by crossing the right side over the left. Declan cranes his neck, trying to see what I'm doing.

I fix him with a look. "Keep still."

He scowls at me but does as he's told. I finish my work of art, then pull the cravat into position against his shirt. I straighten it, turn his collar back down again, then stand back to admire my handiwork.

"There. Will that do?"

He peers in the mirror. "Fuck, that's perfect. Where did you learn to do that?"

"At least some good came of my time at St. Hugh's." I check out Fraze's efforts. His cravat-tying is better than Declan's was, but not up to my standards. "Shall I…?"

"Please do."

Once they are both neatened up, I slip into my lovely dress and turn around for Declan to zip me up. He kisses my shoulder as he does so.

"We're going to have such a good time with you tonight," he murmurs. "Do you want to know what we have planned?"

I swallow, blink at his reflection in the mirror. Behind him, I meet Fraze's gaze, too. "Yes," I reply. "I think I would."

"Well, the spanking's optional, of course. Unless you do something to deserve it, such as being disrespectful or disobedient. But we think you'll be a good girl for us, won't you, Ellie."

My mouth is dry suddenly. I nod. "I will. I'll be a good girl."

"Good girls get to come, and they get fucked. Would you like that?"

"Will it be... I mean, both of you?"

"Oh yes." Fraze takes up the explanation. "Both of us. At the same time."

"What? How ...?"

"Your pussy, your mouth, your arse. We have a choice of three, and only two cocks between us, so there's ample of you to go around."

Ah, yes, I remember now. Declan said something about me sucking a cock whilst the other fucked me. But my arse? I swallow, realign my thoughts to accommodate this new reality, then I straighten my spine and turn to face them both. "That's fine. I can manage that."

"Can you?" Fraze's tone softens. "Yes, I expect you can, and if not, we'll help you."

I manage a small, grateful smile.

Declan shrugs into his jacket, places his top hat on. "Glad we got that settled. So, will I do?"

"You look fabulous," I gush. "Both of you."

Fraze is equally resplendent in his morning suit.

"So do you." Fraze offers me his arm. "There are cocktails and canapés downstairs, and we ought to mingle. Shall we?"

The mingling turns out to be rather easier than I imagined it might be. I do recognise several faces, and one or two of the other guests remember me from school, but of course no one would be impolite enough to mention the unfortunate matter of the maths exam, even if they could call it to mind.

For the most part I am simply one of the guests, companion to the Duke of Erskine and his famous footballer friend. More than a few women send envious looks my way, and who can blame them? I'm with easily the most attractive men here.

That said, the groom comes a close second. Grgur Marek may not be of this social elite, but it seems no one has told him that. He circulates effortlessly among the rich, the famous and the occasionally infamous, chatting to the guests in his perfect and only faintly accented English. He laughs with them, makes jokes, his easy charm and gregarious nature infectious. Fraze observes that it's obvious what Lucy sees in him.

"Good for her," I reply. "A handsome husband who's good company as well. I expect he's great in bed, too."

"I shall make a point of asking Lucy when she comes down?" Fraze sips his cocktail, and I can't miss the wicked glint in his eye. "Not that I want to encourage you to be imagining other men in your bed. Are two not enough?"

"You'll do no such thing," I scold, not sure if he means it or not. "And I wasn't imagining. I just…oh, is that Miranda?"

Fraze's sister was a couple of years older than him so not part of our circle at school. I recognise her at once, though. She always had a more aristocratic bearing than her brother, and none of that has dissipated with the years. At her side is a middle-aged man, attractive in a staid sort of a way. I presume this to be her husband. Their two sons bounce in with them, blond lads aged about ten and twelve I'd say, who head straight for the table laden with cakes and pastries. Their father charges after them whilst Miranda makes a beeline for us.

She kisses her brother on both cheeks, then offers the same greeting to Declan. "I'm so glad you could make it. We don't see enough of you at Hathersmuir. Either of you."

"I know. I'm sorry. Do you remember Ellie, from school?" Fraze draws me forward.

"I don't think so." Miranda furrows her brow, thinking. "Were you on the hockey team?"

"Hardly," I reply, taking her outstretched hand and shaking. "Two left feet, I'm afraid. And the hand-eye coordination of a rabbit."

"Ellie was the brainy type," offers Declan, draping an arm over my shoulders.

Miranda can't miss the possessive gesture. She shrugs as though she's seen all of this before. Perhaps she has. After all, Fraze and Declan have made no secret of the fact that they like to share. Am I one of many she's seen come and go?

"How are things at home?" asks Fraze. He snags a cocktail from a passing waiter and hands it to his sister.

"Good," she replies, "really good, in fact. Opening the house to the public a couple of days a week has brought in a lot of new revenue. I'm thinking of building some holiday lodges and advertising salmon fishing breaks."

Fraze scowls, but his sister is unimpressed. "You might well pull faces, but the place has to pay for itself. Tourism works, there's money in it. You left me to run the estate, and—"

"I know, I know. You're doing a good job. Well, when I say a good job, I mean you're doing okay, I suppose. You'll just have to do what you think best."

She offers an unladylike snort by way of an answer. "Always the know-it-all. Is he this annoying with you, Ellie?"

"What? No. Not at all. I…"

Declan chuckles. "She's teasing you, love. You'll get used to it. These two never stop sparring with each other. The arrangement's simple enough, Miranda runs the estate and Fraze gives her a hard time about it whenever he gets a chance."

I'm still processing all of that when the usher calls us to enter the wedding chapel. It would appear the Honourable Lucinda Sinclair is about to make her entrance.

The day passes in a haze of taffeta, silk, lace, and pretty pink satin bows. Lucy's taste in wedding paraphernalia is very traditional, despite her rather more maverick approach to selecting a husband. The ceremony is uneventful, the food delicious, and the speeches entertaining enough. Several of Grgur's colleagues from the Croatian Philharmonic are here and they rattle off a few traditional waltzes which warm up the room. A Highland band has been hired to lead the serious dancing, complete with a tartan-clad piper. It's all very lively, and I have a wonderful time trying to get my feet around a Scottish jig.

By nine o'clock I'm yawning.

"Ready to go," asks Declan. "Shall we get the car brought round?

"Do we still have our driver?"

"Of course," says Fraze. "He works for the estate. One of the perks of being a duke. Or if you prefer we can stay here. We still have our room upstairs."

I think for a moment, then, "No. If it's all right with you both, I'd prefer to go back to Edinburgh."

"Right. Let's say our goodbyes then and check out."

We had hardly left the grounds of the hotel when I went out like a light. Declan wakes me as we drive through the still lively Edinburgh city centre. I open my eyes to find I've been using his lap as a pillow and feel as though I must have been asleep for hours.

"What time is it?" I ask, my head still groggy.

Declan glances at his watch. "Almost eleven."

He helps me to sit up, and I peer out at the familiar sight of tourists and locals milling along Princes Street. Fraze hands me a bottle of water, and I'm glad of the opportunity to freshen up after consuming more sparkling wine than I'm really used to. Less than two hours after we made our farewells in Pitlochry, Wilson, the liveried chauffeur, pulls up outside Fraze's apartment in Edinburgh. He exits the limousine and opens the rear door for us.

Fraze helps me out, followed by Declan, who pauses for a word with the driver. A couple of twenty-pound notes change hands, and the man hops back into the car and glides back into the traffic.

"If we text Wilson when we're ready to leave, he'll pick us up and take us to the station tomorrow. I told him your luggage can stay in the limo, it'll be safe there."

I'd entirely forgotten that Declan had shoved the case containing half my worldly goods into the boot of the car when we'd left my hotel. "Thank you. It saves having to drag it up the stairs."

"Well, there is a lift," remarks Fraze. "But even so…" He opens the front door and gestures us past him into the entrance hall.

Once back in the apartment I'm not sure whether to go into the lounge or head straight for Fraze's bedroom. Declan settles that question for me by taking my hand and tugging me down the hallway. Once in the bedroom, he tilts his chin toward the huge four-poster. "You're shattered. You can hardly stand up."

"I am tired, yes, but—"

He swirls his finger in the air to tell me to turn around. I do so, and he unzips my dress.

"Get into bed and get some sleep."

"But I thought…"

Fraze has followed us into the room, my artfully tied cravat dangling from his neck, and is already hanging up his jacket. "We both prefer our submissive to be at least semi-conscious when we fuck her. Dec's right. You need to sleep."

My dress is in a pool at my feet. Declan crouches to rescue it as I step out of the matching shoes. I perch on the side of the bed in my underwear, trying to make sense of Fraze's odd choice of words.

"What did you call me? A submissive?"

Bare chested now, he nods at me from across the room. "That's right."

"But, that sounds sort of…subordinate. I don't think—"

"In here, or in any bedroom, actually, that's the way it is between us. We're in charge." He jerks his thumb toward Declan who is also getting undressed. "We give the orders, you do as you're told."

"Well, I know, but I think—"

"It doesn't apply outside. At any other times, we're equals, just three people who respect and care about each other. But in here, when it's just the three of us, Dec and I are both Dominants, which means we get to spank you, to punish you, to fuck you, and your choice is to obey. Or not, but I think you can work out for yourself where that would get you."

"What about my safe word?"

"Good point," agrees Declan. "You wouldn't be punished for using that."

"So, whatever you might say about being Dominants and me being submissive, I'm the one in charge, really. I can call a halt any time I want."

"Smart girl." Fraze strolls toward me in his boxers, his impressive erection tenting the front. "I can see how you got a posh job in one of the best universities and why they sent you to do the talk yesterday. You catch on fast." He pulls back the duvet. "Even smart girls need telling what to do sometimes, and right now you need to sleep. Me, too, actually. Lose the underwear and get in."

Still turning this weird exchange over in my head, I remove my bra and pants. Nude, I scramble under the duvet. Fraze gets in beside me, and Declan, gloriously naked, ambles around to the other side and climbs in, too. I'm glad Fraze saw fit to invest in a bed the size of a swimming pool because there's ample room for all of us, and I feel sort of wonderful sandwiched between both my men. I had assumed they'd be asserting themselves right about now, and I wouldn't have seriously objected, though I am tired. Fraze and Declan have ways of arousing me that I can only dream of, but it seems they're content just to fall into bed alongside me.

I can worry about the submissive thing later. Right now, I need to close my eyes...

CHAPTER EIGHT

I wake feeling much fresher and to the aroma of coffee filling my nostrils. Daylight filters through a crack between the heavy curtains. Fraze is still lying on my right side, face down, his nose buried in his pillow. There's a space on my left, still warm. I'm just considering scooting to the en suite when Declan, clad in just his jeans which he has left unbuttoned, comes back into the room carrying a tray. His hair is wet, slick from the shower. He's brought three mugs of black coffee, a half full bottle of milk, and a plate piled high with buttered toast.

"Wake up, sleeping beauty." He deposits the tray on the bedside table and winks at me, then gives Fraze a not especially gentle nudge.

"Fuck off," comes the muffled reply.

"Suit yourself. I can drink your coffee, eat your share of the toast, and even fuck Ellie all on my own if I have to."

Declan hands me one of the mugs as more expletives can be heard coming from somewhere within the duck down.

Fraze eventually rolls onto his back and cracks open one eye. "How come you're always so chipper in the morning?"

Declan shrugs then sips his coffee. "Must be all those freezing winter dawns I spent as a lad, making up the fires for my betters."

"Bollocks. We had central heating." Fraze manages to sit up, his blond locks beautifully tousled, though he still scowls like a grumpy teenager. He turns to me. "Morning, beautiful."

"Good morning," I reply, hugging the duvet to my naked breasts with one hand as I manage my cup with the other. I smile at Declan. "And thanks for the breakfast."

"You're welcome. Toast?" Declan passes me the plate, and I select a piece. It's dripping with melted butter. Delicious!

Declan also selects a slice and lounges across the foot of the bed to eat it.

"You two are getting crumbs everywhere," grumbles our host, but even so he, too, grabs a slice and starts tucking in.

"What time's our train?" I enquire, two slices of toast later.

Declan dusts crumbs from his fingers onto the carpet. "There's one every hour. You did say you have an open return ticket, didn't you?"

"Yes."

"No problem, then. We'll leave when we're ready. Are you working tomorrow?"

"I should be. I'm usually in my lab by eight o'clock."

"I'm due at our training ground by ten in the morning. What about you?" Declan directs his question to Fraze.

"I've a client meeting in the City but not until lunchtime."

"Plenty of time to spend half the day in bed, then. We can catch a train this afternoon."

A quiver of excited anticipation snakes through me, reigniting my urge to use the bathroom. "Er, could I just... I mean, I thought I might have a shower. Clean my teeth..."

Fraze is also finishing his breakfast and plants a kiss on my mouth. I taste the rich tang of coffee on his breath.

"Feel free. I brought your overnight bag in, so your stuff's to hand. There's a shower in the en suite and another down the hall." He quirks an eyebrow at Declan. "I assume you already made use of it?"

"Yeah." Declan rakes his fingers through his hair, still damp. "I got up early." He starts to collect together the debris from our breakfast and piles it all back onto the tray. "You two get sorted while I collect together a few bits and pieces."

"What sort of bits and pieces?" I squeak.

"You'll see. Go on, unless you want one of us to wash your back. Come to think of it..."

"No, no, I'll be fine." I drop the duvet and scramble from the bed, self-conscious about my nudity despite our intimacies of two nights ago and despite having slept between them last night.

By sheer force of will, I manage not to dash across the room to the en suite, maintaining a dignified pace and what I hope passes for a suggestive sway of my hips.

I emerge thirty minutes later swathed in a huge navy-blue bath sheet and feeling decidedly fresher. My teeth are brushed, my hair still wet but clean and sleek, courtesy of the comb I found in the bathroom cabinet along with the toothpaste. I helped myself to Fraze's shampoo and expensive body wash.

They are both in the bedroom, Declan stretching out on the bed which has been straightened after our night together, and Fraze is lounging in a chair by the window. Fraze now has a towel around his waist but that's all. His naked male torso is every bit as impressive as Declan's, pectoral muscles clearly defined and a solid six pack. Declan is still wearing just his black jeans, and his bare chest is equally stunning. Years of professional sports training will do that, I suppose. On the duvet next to him are a pile of condoms, a butt plug, and a tube of lubricant

I take in the sight. This must be what he meant by a few bits and pieces. "I don't suppose you have a hairdryer," I enquire tentatively.

Fraze shrugs. "'Fraid not. We'll get one for the next time you're here."

"Thank you." I stand awkwardly in the centre of the room and look from one man to the other. "Should I…?"

"Come here." Declan beckons me to him and shifts so that I can sit on the bed. "Kneel in front of me, facing away."

I obey.

"Pass me a towel, would you?"

Fraze gets to his feet and fetches one of the smaller blue towels from the shower room. He balls it up then tosses it to Declan.

"Thanks." Declan drapes the towel over my head and starts to pat my hair dry, squeezing the excess moisture from my damp locks. His fingers are firm, massaging my scalp with authority and skill. I close my eyes and tilt back my head to better enjoy his ministrations. I'm nervous, for sure. I know what's coming. That butt plug tells its own story, and anal sex will be a massive first for me. The sight of the lube, too, fills me with trepidation, but for some reason the moment either one of them lays a hand on me, I melt.

Eventually Declan sets the damp towel aside and produces a hairbrush from the bedside table. He turns it over in his hands.

"You know, this is a paddle brush. As the name suggests, it packs a fair punch when applied to a bare bottom. Would you like to try it?"

My stomach clenches, and my pussy starts to leak. I manage to nod, not trusting myself to actually get the words out.

"Okay. First your hair, then your bottom. Agreed?"

"Yes," I manage. "Agreed."

"Ellie, do you remember our conversation yesterday, just before we got into bed?" This from Fraze, who has been watching Declan dry my hair for me. At my nod, he continues. "We explained that here, in the bedroom, we're the Dominants, Doms if you prefer, and you're the submissive."

"Yes, I remember."

"Okay. Well that means you need to be a little more respectful. You can start by calling us Sir when we're in a scene or when you're being punished."

"Sir? You want me to call you Sir? Like at school?" I gape at him, uncertain what to make of this. I did my research and I came across this terminology, but the reality still catches me unawares.

Fraze chuckles, but his expression is deadly serious. "Not exactly like at school, but yes. Sir will do fine. Any problems with that?"

"Is this to do with you being a duke?" Even as I say it, I know that's a silly question.

"It has to do with me and Dec being your Doms. A sub is always polite, always respectful, and that means you refer to us as Sir. There's more, and if you find the role of our submissive is one you like, then we can teach you the rest. We'll take it a bit at a time, though, and we'll be satisfied with this for now. Are we clear?"

I consider what he's said for a few moments. If I'm honest with myself, there were a few times during our more intense scenes when I could so easily have said something along those lines anyway. It would have seemed natural and right. I suppose it has to do with the time and the place. And the men.

"Yes," I murmur.

"Yes what, Ellie," prompts Fraze, softly.

"Yes, Sir."

Declan kisses my bare shoulder. "A fast learner. So, your hair..."

He draws the brush through my moist locks, arranging each one against my neck. When he finishes, he nuzzles my earlobe.

"Lose the towel, Ellie," he commands, "then you can lie across my lap. Or Fraze's, if you prefer."

I glance over at Fraze who has made himself pretty comfortable, his bare feet propped on a low, padded stool. His grin is sensual, pure lust. "Go ahead, I'm good here. You redden her arse, then I'll have some fun with the butt plug. Agreed?"

"Sounds fair enough." Declan turns so he is now sitting on the side of the bed, the hairbrush ready in his hand. "Hurry up, girl. Once you've been given an instruction, we don't like to be kept waiting."

Another rule I have to learn, I suppose. I unwrap the towel from around myself and leave it on the bed when I stand up and move around to get in position. Without being told, I go to Declan's right side. He's right-handed, so I expect he'll prefer that, and it gives Fraze an unrestricted view of my backside.

When did I become so considerate?

"Are you ready?"

"Yes," I reply, my bottom bared and suitably up-ended to receive the flat side of the hairbrush. I'm not sure how much this is going to sting, but I suspect it'll be a lot.

"Have you forgotten your manners already?" Declan taps my buttock with the brush

"Yes, Sir," I correct myself, clenching.

There is no further preamble. The hairbrush connects with my left buttock, and the sound of the slap reverberates around the room. It's loud, shockingly loud, a sharp crack which echoes and fills the space surrounding us.

"Ow," I squeal. "Shit, that hurts."

"Yeah? Fancy that." Declan slaps me again, and I wriggle on his lap.

I can feel his erection nudging my hip. At least one of us is enjoying themselves.

He tightens his grip around my waist, pulling me in close to him, and he traps my legs under one of his to hold me still. The next few swats are rapid, and my bottom is on fire. I let out a grunt with each slap, my sounds rising to a scream as the heat builds.

"Stop! That's enough…please…"

"Safe word or shut up." The curt command comes from Fraze.

I settle for cursing under my breath as I have a feeling that if I actually swear at them they'll consider it disrespectful and my problems will get worse.

"Are you muttering, Ellie?" Declan pauses to speak to me.

"No, Sir," I grind out. "Not muttering."

"Nothing to say, then?"

"No, Sir."

Declan caresses my smarting backside, and I wince as the pain seeps into my flesh and tissues. Then the spanking starts up again. I scream, squirm about as much as I am able to, but some inner demon prevents me from stopping it all by shouting 'red'. I manage to ride the pain somehow, allow it to fill me and expand right out to my fingers and toes. There is something beautifully cleansing about being hurt in this way, liberating even. This is my choice, this deliberate loss of self and of control. I am in their hands and want to be nowhere else.

I almost don't notice when Declan stops. The pain is everywhere, in every crack and cranny, as though he has reached in and mastered every part of me. I lie, motionless, breathing slowly, deeply, as my body throbs.

"That was beautiful, Ellie. Thank you." It's Fraze who speaks to me, and he's close. Very close.

I open my eyes as he scoops my almost dry hair back from my face and view him through a haze of tears. I hadn't even realised I was crying.

"Spread your legs, little sub. We want to know how wet you are."

I do as he tells me. Moisture seeps from my pussy, and I know I must have made Declan's jeans wet, too, though he doesn't seem to mind.

"I'm sorry. I…have I made a mess?"

"You can wash them for me later." Declan leans to the side to get a better view. "Shit, so swollen and fucking soaked." He thrusts two fingers into my pussy. "Tight, too. Our slut certainly loves to be spanked."

"She does, and look how red her arse is. Fucking gorgeous. Nice job, bro."

Fraze uses his fingers to part the two stinging globes of my arse, then runs his hand through my sodden folds. He wipes his palm on my buttocks, and I cry out as the heat sizzles again. "I think she's ready."

They are no longer talking to me, but over me, about me, as though I wasn't here. It's humiliating, but acutely sexy, too. My erotic horizons are expanding by the day, by the hour almost. I can only manage a low moan as Declan plunges his fingers in and out a couple more times, then withdraws them. Fraze helps me to stand up straight.

"She's very wet, but we'll still use plenty of lube. Pass me it, will you?"

Declan picks up the tube, squirts a generous coating of it onto the butt plug, then tosses the tube to Fraze.

"Kneel on the bed, head and shoulders down and arse as high as you can lift it. And you'll need to spread your legs, too, as wide as you can." Fraze issues his commands in a stern, no-nonsense voice, and I hurry to obey.

"So pretty." Fraze parts my buttocks again to examine my tight rear hole. "Shall we see if we can loosen this up a bit? I'm going to fuck her with the plug first, then my cock."

"Sounds like a plan," Declan agrees. "I've lubed up the plug for you."

"Thanks."

I let out a squeal as the cool gel hits my arsehole.

"Hush," admonishes Fraze. "You're going to accept this without making a fuss. You know that I won't harm you."

"I'm sorry, Sir."

I manage to remain still when Fraze starts to work an oiled finger into my rear hole. It feels odd, very intimate, and my humiliation is absolute, but it's not painful.

"Would you like Dec to stroke your clit while I'm doing this?"

Christ, that sounds wonderful. "Yes, please, Sir."

"Ask him, then. Ask him very nicely and he might."

I turn my head to face Declan. "Please, Sir, would you stroke my clit."

"Why?"

"B-because it would feel nice, Sir." I grimace when Fraze pushes his finger fully inside me. "Please…"

"Would you come all over my hand, like a sloppy little sub with no self-control?"

"I'll try not to, Sir."

"Good, because you don't get to come until this plug is fully in and Fraze is fucking your arse with it. Do you understand?"

"Yes, Sir."

He quirks his lip and moves to sit beside me. The slick plug is still in his hand, and he uses that to press against my clit, then slowly rubs back and forth. The sensation is amazing. My pussy starts to convulse.

"No tightening up." Fraze taps my bottom. "Keep this nice and slack for me."

"Sorry, Sir." I try to relax, while moaning at the intense waves of pleasure that Declan is creating. My arousal blossoms, then starts to spike. "Sir, you need to stop…"

Declan pauses, and I manage to regain some semblance of control. My arse feels tight and very wet. I can hear the sounds as Fraze pumps two fingers in and out, then he drives his digits deep and scissors them inside me to stroke my inner walls.

I gasp. It feels lewd, dirty and forbidden, but utterly wonderful, too.

"She's ready. Pass me the plug."

Fraze's fingers leave my body, and I feel suddenly bereft. Empty. The nudge of the plug at my entrance is comforting.

"Push back and let the plug go in."

I manage to comply with Fraze's softly spoken advice, but still it burns when the ring of muscle stretches to take the widest part of the plug. It's thicker than Fraze's two fingers were. I let out a nervous little whimper, but suddenly the pain is gone and the plug slips into place.

I feel incredibly full, stretched, crammed to bursting. But I'm okay. More than okay. I want more.

Fraze slowly draws the plug out. He stops when the widest part is again stretching me wide open, then he twists the plug and dribbles more lube around it before shoving it deep again.

I moan. The sensation is beautifully erotic, achingly intimate. I yearn for Declan's fingers.

"Please, Sir…my clit?"

Declan chuckles. "Such a demanding, horny little sub. Are you wanting to come, Ellie?"

Yes! Fraze drags the plug back and forth. I manage a nod and punctuate each stroke with a sharp grunt. My entrance is stretched to the point of pain, but it's a wonderful hurting. My powers of communication are somewhat lacking, but Declan understands what I need, and he reaches for me. He rolls my throbbing nub between his fingers, and at the same time Fraze pumps the plug in and out, gathering speed now as my arse opens to accept the intrusion.

My arousal swells and threatens to overwhelm me. I recall something about asking permission.

"Please, I want to come. I need to come…"

"Okay." Fraze inserts the plug hard and twists it inside me. "Go ahead."

My orgasm erupts. I thrust back against Fraze, seeking more friction, more of everything. He uses his fingers to circle my stretched arse each time he pulls the plug out, sending more waves of pleasure pulsing through my body. The sensation ripples through me, a hot flood of thrilling, stunning intensity. I'm drowning in it, floating on it, weightless and sinking at the same time.

The feelings ebb. I sink forward and start to roll to my side. Declan catches me and pulls me into his arms so I am lying face-down on his chest. The plug is still lodged within me.

"You okay, sweetheart?" Declan nuzzles my hair.

"Yes," I murmur. "Yes, Sir. Thank you."

"You were made for anal sex, Ellie. You did well, and your response was fucking awesome." Fraze taps the protruding finger grip on the plug, and another ripple of sensation flutters the length of my rear channel.

"Oh! Oh, wow."

"Did you like it?" Fraze asks me.

"I must have, I suppose. I came after all."

"That's not the same thing. We can do all sorts of things to you that'll make you come. Some of them you won't like but you won't be able to control your response. Anal sex could be like that for you, a sure-fire trigger for an orgasm, but you still might not like it."

I think about that for a few moments and I sort of understand what he means. "I did like it, Sir. Once I got over being embarrassed, and especially when Declan stroked my clit, too."

"I reckon we can get her to do just about anything if we stroke her clit at the same time."

I groan. Declan's probably spot on about that.

"You're tolerating that medium-sized plug well enough, so I want to try you with a bigger one." Fraze gets up and heads over to a chest of drawers. He's deposited the towel somewhere so is now gloriously naked, his erect cock reaching almost to his navel. He finds what he wants in the top drawer and returns to the bed, then shows me the monster butt plug he has in his hand. "As you can see, this one's the same width as a cock, so once you've accepted this, the rest will be plain sailing. Yes?"

I gulp. "I... I suppose so, Sir."

He grins at me. "Back in position, then. I'll remove the one you have in your arse, and Dec can insert this one."

"I'm not sure I'm ready. What if—?"

Declan tips up my chin with his fingers. "You have your safe word. If it's too much you just say 'red' and I'll stop. And I'll be gentle, I promise."

I blink up at him, then nod. My safe word, right. I scramble back onto my knees. "So, do I just bend over, like before?"

"That's right." Declan is already squirting lube onto the large plug. "I think she might need more of this inside, too."

"Sure." Fraze jerks his finger to indicate I need to get in position now.

I obey, conscious that the bright red silicone finger grip is sticking out of my arse.

Fraze takes hold of it and pulls it out, slowly, deliberately. I hold my breath until the toy exits my body, then watch him squirt lube onto the snub nose. Next, he applies more to my rear entrance. He aligns the freshly lubed plug and slides it back into me. It enters with ease this time, and I am encouraged by that. He swirls it around, jabs it back and forth a couple of times, then pulls it out again.

Declan switches places with Fraze. He places the head of the larger plug at my entrance. "Same as before, push back and try to relax."

Fraze strolls across the room toward the en suite, the discarded plug in his hand. "I'll just get rid of this, then I'll help you if you need it."

I'm dimly aware of the sound of running water as Fraze washes his hands. The new plug already feels a lot bigger, and I'm not sure I can manage it after all.

Declan knows better. He presses gently but firmly, and my entrance parts to allow the new plug to penetrate the ring of furled muscle. The copious amount of lube helps. The toy is slippery, and once the first inch is inside the rest follows. My arsehole is stretched impossibly wide, the burning sensation back with a vengeance. I grasp handfuls of the duvet, panting, then I almost sob with gratitude when Fraze's deft fingers caress my clit. He strokes, drawing his fingertip over the top of the sensitive nubbin, then squeezing gently. It feels exquisite, and I almost don't notice when Declan resumes the pressure and the huge plug finally settles inside me.

"Good girl," Declan murmurs. "Now, I'll just work it in and out a bit, help you to get used to it."

Oh, God. I clench, unable to help myself.

"Relax, sweetheart. I promised to be gentle."

And he is. Declan slowly draws the plug out, then slides it forward again, his movements smooth and achingly gentle. After three or four thrusts, I'm starting to believe this is going to be okay after all. That opinion is reinforced by Fraze's feather-light caresses. He strokes my clit and the folds of my pussy lips, and my arousal is spiking again.

"I think I want to come. May I…?"

"Not this time." Declan's tone is hard, curt even. He expects to be obeyed.

"But I need to come. I can't—"

"You need to hold it, until we're both inside you. Then you can come as much as you want."

I'm confused. What does Declan mean? Both inside me?

Declan pulls the plug out so the widest part is again stretching me. "Does that hurt?"

"Yes," I manage. "Yes, it hurts, Sir."

"How much? On a scale of one to ten?"

"F-five, Sir. Perhaps six."

He twists the plug and dribbles more lube onto it. "Is it getting better? Or worse?"

"B-better, Sir. Maybe four."

"I think she's ready." He slides the toy right inside me, then draws it out again to the fattest point. He repeats the action several times, then asks me again. "Better, or worse?"

"Better, Sir. It's fine." I think…

He pushes the plug fully inside until it's seated snugly, the bulbous shape stretching my inner walls.

Fraze stops stroking me and leans back on his elbows. "Straighten up, Ellie."

"I'm not sure I can move, Sir."

"Yes, you can. Just take it slow."

Gingerly, I use my arms to push myself upright. The plug shifts inside me, but it's not painful. I manage a tremulous smile, inordinately pleased with myself.

Declan grabs one of the condoms from the small pile he dumped on the bed. He unzips his jeans and kicks them off, then sheaths himself. Never one to miss an opportunity, I take a good look this time. His cock is every bit as jaw-droppingly awesome as Fraze's, standing proudly upright as he lies back on the bed.

"Straddle him," commands Fraze, "then lower yourself onto his cock."

I gape at him. "I don't think I can. It'll be too much…"

"You don't know that until you try." Fraze holds out his hand. "I'll help steady you."

I do as I'm told, but slowly. Neither of them is in any hurry, it seems. They wait until I manage to lift my leg over Declan's hips. In this position his cock is right at my entrance. I watch him fist the shaft and angle his cock to ease my penetration.

"When you're ready, girl," he murmurs, and winks at me.

I rest my hands on Declan's shoulders and start to lower myself. The crown of his cock slips easily into my drooling, welcoming pussy, but the plug in my arse shifts with the pressure. It feels incredible, so tight, so impossibly full.

Fraze is behind me, his hands on my hips. He doesn't push or hurry me, but he helps to support my weight as I drop lower, then lower still. Declan's cock is almost fully inside me when, gasping, I stop.

"I'm not sure…"

"Breathe, Ellie. In, then out." Declan smooths my hair back from my face. "In, then out. That's right. Again."

Under his gentle encouragement, I get over my crisis of confidence. The final inch is relatively easy, and I find myself perched on his hips, impaled on his cock, his dark pubic hair tickling the tender skin of my bottom.

"Good girl." Declan closes his eyes, his lips twisting into a sensual grimace. "Fuck, that's so tight. It feels incredible."

"Yes," I whisper. "Yes, it does."

I squeeze my pussy around him, and he gyrates his hips to grind his cock deeper.

"Lean forward, Ellie," he growls, "and kiss me."

I cradle his jaw in both my hands and do as he instructs. He tangles his fingers through my hair, spearing his tongue into my mouth. I join in the sensual dance with my own tongue, twisting it around his. Eventually Declan breaks the kiss.

"Fraze is going to take the plug out now, and then you'll take his cock in your arse."

I know my eyes widen, I'm still not clear how this will all work, or even if it's possible at all, though they both seem perfectly confident. Still, the choreography of it eludes me.

Fraze is already rolling a condom over his dick. That done, he takes hold of the finger grip on the plug and pulls gently.

My body is curiously reluctant to give up the toy, but the struggle is an unequal one, and the plug exits rather more easily than it went in. Moments later, the head of Fraze's cock is nudging my now wide-open entrance. He drives forward, and the crown slides past the sphincter.

I groan. His cock is no wider than the plug, but it's a whole lot longer. The stretching doesn't stop. It continues, inexorable, becoming sharper. The burning is more intense as he pushes farther forward, filling my arse inch by painful inch.

"Look at me, sweetheart." Declan cups my chin, his face close, his beautiful dark eyes caring. "Don't look away. Eyes on me, and you know you can do it."

"Please, can you help me…?"

He smiles. "Of course, you only have to ask." He slides his hand between our bodies to find my clit, then takes it between his fingers and tugs gently. "How's that?"

"Wonderful, Sir."

He breaks eye contact with me to glance at Fraze. "She's okay now. You can carry on."

So Fraze does. He drives the rest of his cock balls deep into my slick and well-prepared arse, then both men hold still, allowing me to adjust to the incredible pressure and feeling of fullness. I let out a ragged breath, scared to move, convinced I'll split in two.

"You're beautiful, you know that, Ellie. We always thought so. Strong, brave, brilliant." Declan's softly whispered words sink into my soul, replenish my courage as he continues to caress my clit. "We should never have let you slip away from us."

"I missed you so much, Sir… Sirs."

Fraze kisses the nape of my neck, then slowly slides his cock back, almost all the way out. He drives it deep again, slowly, smoothly, and I sigh, though in contentment now. This feels wrong yet so totally right. Incredibly, my arousal is blossoming again.

Fraze withdraws then thrusts again, but this time when he drives his cock back into me, Declan withdraws his. They set up a rhythm, alternating their thrusts, one plunging deep as the other pulls out. My senses are reeling under the onslaught, my body filled to capacity. My inner walls are stretched tight around two cocks, the friction in both my channels beyond exquisite.

"Oh, God," I moan.

"Are we hurting you?"

I shake my head in response to Declan's concerned question. "It feels wonderful, Sir. I can't believe…I never imagined…"

He brushes his lips over mine, then lays back against the pillow. I lay my cheek on his chest, drinking in the riot of sensual bliss as they fuck me in unison.

"I think…may I come, Sir?"

I'm not sure who I'm asking, but it's Fraze who answers.

"Of course, sweetheart."

Declan increases the pressure on my clit, and they speed up their combined fucking. White light again explodes behind my eyes. Juices drip from my pussy. I'm floating, carried along on a surge of pure lust, my pussy and arse convulsing. Ripples of delight course through me. Moments after my orgasm, Declan lets out a low growl, and his cock lurches inside my cunt.

Fraze isn't far behind. He mutters something which sounds like 'holy fuck', then rams his cock deep and holds still. His semen jets forth to fill the condom with wet heat.

CHAPTER NINE

"These seats will do." Declan shoulders my case and
pushes it up onto the overhead rack, then gestures me into the
window seat.

We're on the five o'clock train from Edinburgh to
Kings Cross, again enjoying the luxury of the first-class
carriage. The train is already filling up with business people
heading back to London in readiness for the working week.
We're lucky to find an empty table.

We had a very late lunch at an Italian trattoria close to
the apartment so we decided not to buy any food for the journey.
In any case, there's always the buffet car. Fraze texted Wilson
from the restaurant, and the chauffeur picked us up outside. He
dropped the three of us, Declan's holdall, and my monster of a
case off at the station entrance a couple of minutes later.

We make ourselves at home, our travel cups of
Starbucks lattes on the table in front of us. This time Declan sits
opposite me, and Fraze is at my side. For the first few miles
we're all three of us content to sip our coffees and watch the
scenery rush past us. It's not until we're leaving Berwick-upon-
Tweed that Fraze leans forward, one elbow on the table.

"So, Ellie. It was a stroke of luck meeting you on the
way up here. Have you had a good weekend?"

"Christ, yes! The best."

"So, you'd do it again?"

"Come back to Edinburgh, you mean?"

"Not necessarily. We want to carry on seeing you, in
London, if that suits you. Or you could come to Hatfield. Or
Peterborough."

"I'd love to," I blurt. "I mean, I sort of assumed that we would."

Declan grins from across the table. "We assumed that, too, but it's always good to check. In a relationship like ours, it's important to be clear, to say what you want, what you expect."

"A relationship like ours? You mean, because there are two of you and one of me?"

"There is that, obviously. But it's more the Dom-sub thing that I was thinking of. That's where the trust and honesty comes in."

I glance about nervously, but even though the train is fairly crowded, there are no other passengers within earshot.

"I know, but do we have to discuss it here? I mean, someone might hear, and—"

"And what? We're consenting adults." Declan reaches for my hand. "But don't worry, Ellie. We're just as keen on discretion as you are, perhaps more as we're both in the public eye. We're not ashamed of what we do, how we like to have fun, but it's not everyone's cup of tea, and no one's business but ours. And now yours. Obviously."

"Yes, so could we have this conversation somewhere more private?"

"Absolutely. I just needed to establish that we would be having the conversation." Declan leans back. "So, lovely Ellie. You know a lot about both of us. How about you fill us in on some of the details of your life and what's been happening since school? You come from somewhere in Yorkshire originally. Is that right?"

"Yes, Leeds. My father still lives there. My mum died of cancer two years ago."

"That's tough." Fraze squeezes my hand. "My mother died when I was quite young, too. Were you close?"

I nod. "I still miss her every day, although I don't know what she would have made of all this."

Fraze adopts an expression of mock indignation. "What's to object to? I'm a peer of the realm, and although you wouldn't know it to look at him, Dec's a sporting icon. National treasures, both of us."

I laugh. "Idiot."

Fraze scowls at me. "Is that any way to address your Dom?"

"Idiot, Sir," I amend.

He seems to accept that. "I'd like to meet your father sometime."

I think I might like that, too.

A couple of hours later we're pulling out of Wakefield when the ticket inspector makes his rounds. He checks our travel documents.

"Kings Cross," he remarks as he draws a squiggly line on my ticket and hands it back to me. "Peterborough," he observes when he checks Declan's ticket, and the same for Fraze's.

"I want to stay on as far as London, though," says Fraze. "Can I buy the extra ticket from you?"

"It's the same price, sir," replies the inspector, "but I'll need to issue you a ticket for the barriers at Kings Cross." He taps some buttons on the machine slung around his neck, then hands Fraze the additional ticket. "Enjoy the rest of your journey, sir."

"Not headed for home, then?" Declan eyes Fraze from the seat opposite.

"No. I'll check into the Four Seasons. It'll be handier for my meeting tomorrow, saves commuting in on Monday morning."

"Fair enough. Pricey, though. That's one of the best hotels in London."

"You can stay at my flat," I blurt. "If you like, I mean. It's not up to five-star standards and not so convenient, perhaps, but it's okay, and you'd be welcome."

Fraze gazes at me, his head tilted to one side. Declan, too, lifts an eyebrow. Have I said the wrong thing? I really don't have a clue about the rules of this threesome thing I've gotten into.

Fraze narrows his eyes. "That's very kind of you, Ellie. Are you sure?"

"Yes, of course. If that's okay with Declan, obviously. I mean, unless I'm only supposed to be with you both at the same time?"

"Seems we need to have at least some of that conversation now," observes Declan. "You see, Ellie, from our point of view, if this thing between us is going to go anywhere, this relationship has to be exclusive. That means you belong to us. No one else."

"Of course. I get that."

"Both of us equally, either together or separately. Here's the way of it. I'm often busy at weekends, especially in the soccer season. Fraze has to make frequent business trips, and they're as often as not mid-week. So you see, if we were to insist you only play with both of us together, you'd be alone a lot of the time, and that's not reasonable, is it?"

"I suppose not, although…"

Fraze takes up the explanation. "So, if you and I are both free on a weekend while Dec's away, we should get together if we want. Over the years we've both come to like this double Dom dynamic, but one-on-one fucking is pretty damn good, too."

I don't say so, but it certainly sounds perfectly acceptable to me.

Fraze lets that point settle before he continues. "And if I'm away when he's available, you and Dec could keep each other company if that's what you want to do. We're exclusive, but to each other. You don't fuck anyone unless it's one of us."

"And what about you?"

"Me?" Fraze frowns at me.

"Both of you. If I don't fuck anyone else, neither should you. Either of you."

"Absolutely." Fraze smiles and inclines his head

"Agreed," says Declan. "Goes without saying."

"Have you ever done this before? Shared a girlfriend, I mean?"

"You're our sub, not our girlfriend," Fraze corrects. "A sub is a whole lot more than just a woman to fuck. I know a girlfriend is, too, or can be, but at least in my experience this is much closer. Much more trust and intimacy is required. It's a big deal."

"Okay, sorry." I rephrase my question. "Have you shared a sub before?"

"We've played in threesomes, in clubs as a rule. There's never been a sub who we both clicked with in such a major way, though. Even after just a couple of days together, you're special to us. We already talked about it, about you, and we want to make this work long term. I think we both knew that right from the start."

"Yeah," Declan agrees. "Chemistry."

"Long term? Like a marriage almost?"

Declan shrugs. "I suppose so. A lot like that but without the public vows. In our lifestyle there are ways of showing commitment, and who knows? Maybe you'll wear our collar in the future."

I take that in for a few moments, then turn to Fraze. "But what about your family? Don't you need to marry some honourable lady and produce lots of little dukes?"

Fraze quirks his lip, shaking his head. "We're not in the middle ages now, though I suppose the British aristocracy has some way to go before we actually join the twenty-first century. The royals are ahead of us for once. The Law of Succession was changed a couple of years ago to give girls the same rights as boys."

He's lost me. "Sorry, what do you mean?"

"The law was changed so now the eldest child of the monarch inherits the crown, whether male or female. If that same logic applied to the aristocracy, Miranda would be Duchess of Erskine and I'd be just a humble lord."

"I can't imagine you being a humble anything."

"Thank you. I'll take that as a compliment."

"But don't you…?"

"Need an heir? Yes, obviously. But you saw those two hooligans with Miranda at Pitlochry. Didn't they look to you like an heir and a spare?"

"Well I suppose so, but…"

"If I die without any children of my own, Alistair, Miranda's eldest boy, will be the next duke, and that suits me fine. I'll live my life the way I want to, and Hathersmuir will manage perfectly well. Miranda's in charge there anyway, she'll teach the lad all he needs to know."

"But don't you care about, well…?"

"Preserving the dynasty? Of course, and if it wasn't for Miranda I'd have to step up and apply myself. But this way's fine, everybody's happy, and I get to fuck who I like, the way I like."

"Not to mention, he's not buried somewhere in the glens with just Highland cattle and thistles for company," observes Declan. "I've always said he'd make a rubbish laird. Monarch of the Glen, I don't think so."

"Fuck off," retorts Fraze, though with no trace of acrimony. I get the impression this is another of their private jokes rehearsed over the years and now shared with me.

I smile to myself and settle back in my seat. There are interesting times ahead.

*****

"Sir, that feels good. So good..."

Declan's arms tighten around my waist. Steadied, I bounce up and down on his beautiful cock. He takes my engorged nipple in his mouth and sucks hard, making me scream with pleasure.

The disruptive trill of a phone halts me in mid-downward stroke.

Declan releases my turgid peak to glance up at me. "That's mine. Ignore it."

"What if it's important?"

"This is important," he grunts. "Don't fucking stop."

"No, Sir." I sink down to impale myself fully again. "Sir, may I...?"

"Go ahead," he growls.

I slide my hand between our bodies to find my clit and I rub hard. My orgasm, already smouldering, threatening to ignite, now bursts into flames. I cling to Declan, my free arm wrapped around his neck as he thrusts his cock upwards to spear me. The crown bumps against my cervix, and my climax erupts.

When my frantic shudders start to ebb, Declan grasps me under my buttocks, causing me to squeal again as the freshly spanked skin is still very tender. He rolls us both over so now I find myself looking up at him while he pounds his cock into my pussy. He delivers several deep, driving strokes, then withdraws and realigns at the entrance to my arse. I lift my hips and try to relax, to be slack for him.

His penetration is slow, smooth and practised. He lubed me first with his fingers so I'm ready and receptive. I grope for my clit when he increases the tempo, fucking my arse with deep, determined strokes. This time we come together, a hot, sweaty climax which leaves both of us panting.

At last Declan withdraws and rolls onto his back beside me. "Fucking wonderful, girl."

"Thank you, Sir. You, too."

This is one of those occasions when it's just the two of us. Fraze is in the U.S., not due back for a couple of days. Declan picked me up from the lab, which caused a bit of a stir among the students. We went for something to eat, then came back to my flat. I'm hoping he'll be able to stay for a night or two, then when Fraze returns…

It's been nearly six months now, and our arrangement suits me very well. I see one or the other of them several times a week, and when all three of us are together the sex is every bit as explosive as it was in Edinburgh. It never pales, the intoxicating thrill of being the centre of their attention never fades.

I adore them. I love them both with a passion I could hardly imagine let alone articulate. I've never been happier.

"Would you like a coffee, Sir?" I prop myself up on my elbow and gaze down at my gorgeous dark-haired Dom.

"Love one. On your way would you pass me my phone? It's in my jeans pocket."

I scramble from the bed and scoot around to the foot where Declan's jeans are strewn in a heap on the floor with the rest of our clothes.

The phone starts to ring again as soon as I pick it up. "Someone's keen to get hold of you." I hand it to him and hope he's not being summoned to some extra training session which would mean he has to cut short his visit.

He glances at the number displayed on the screen. "It's Miranda," he tells me. "Wonder what she wants…"

I leave the room as he answers the call.

"Hi. How are you?"

When I trot back in with two cups of coffee, Declan has his jeans and socks back on and is just buttoning his shirt.

"Oh." My heart sinks. "Are you going?"

"I have to get back to Scotland. My mum had an accident, a car crash. She's in intensive care at Inverness."

"Oh no! How bad is it?"

"Miranda didn't know all the details. A collapsed lung and internal bleeding, apparently, but they're still doing tests. She thought I should get back there."

"Of course. What can I do to help?"

"I'm not sure. I just—"

"You'll need a flight to Inverness. I'll go online and book it while you get your stuff together."

He just nods. I slip into a robe and head back to the kitchen where my laptop is set up on the counter. The next available flight is in two hours. I select one seat, then think better of it and change that to two. There's no way I'm letting Declan face whatever's waiting for him alone. Fraze would be with him if he were here, but he isn't, so…

My next task is to phone a cab company and book a car to the airport. I'm assured it'll be outside in twenty minutes

Back in the bedroom, Declan is flinging stuff into his trusty bright orange holdall. I grab my own overnight bag from the top of my wardrobe.

"The flight's in two hours. I booked a taxi to the airport. You do have photo ID on you, don't you?"

"Er, yes. My driving licence. What are you doing, Ellie?"

"I'm packing. I'm coming with you."

He regards me in silence for several moments then nods just once. "Good. I'm glad. Thank you."

The trip to the airport is tense. Declan phones Miranda back to let her know our plans and that I'll be coming to Scotland with him. She's at the hospital with his mother and tells him there's been no change, his mother has yet to regain consciousness, and there's been no further news from the medics. I gather she offered to have a room made ready for me at Hathersmuir, but Declan tells her that won't be necessary as I'll be sharing his.

"I have an apartment in the main house. So does Fraze, though neither of us have actually lived there for years now. Miranda insists."

"That's generous of her. And did you say your mother lives on the estate, too?"

He nods. "She has a cottage about a mile from the main house. The old duke left it to her in his will, and she always intended to retire there. I just hope…"

I reach for his hand. "She'll be back there soon. I know it."

"Christ, I hope so."

I squeeze his hand again and leave him to his thoughts while I text Fraze.

Allannah had an accident. In hospital, Inverness. We're flying up there now.

He replies at once. *How bad?*

Not sure. Miranda's with her. It sounds serious.

A few minutes pass, then he texts me again.

Just spoke to M. No change since she spoke to Dec. I'll be there tomorrow.

Are you cutting your trip short?

Too right I am!

Less than four hours after Declan took Miranda's call, we're landing at Inverness. It's almost two o'clock in the morning when we emerge from the terminal building to find Wilson waiting for us at the gate. He explains that Miranda sent him and offers to drive us to Hathersmuir if we want to freshen up and get a few hours' sleep, or straight to the hospital.

"The hospital, please." Declan helps the driver to sling our bags in the boot, then follows me into the rear seat.

Intensive care is a twenty-four seven business, and no one there turns a hair when we show up in the middle of the night. The nurse who opens the electronic door to admit us to the ward points to a bay at the far end. I recognise a white-faced Miranda perched on the plastic seat beside the high bed. She stands as we hurry down the ward, and Declan takes her in a firm hug.

"Thank you for calling me. And for being here."

"She's always been like a mother to me, and to Iain. Where else would I be?" She lifts her hand in greeting to me. "Hello again."

"Hello," I reply. "Has there been any change?"

Declan releases Miranda, and she shakes her head. "No, but at least she's stable."

On the bed a small woman lies motionless, a tube inserted into her throat through her mouth. A huge bundle of lines and wires connect her to a range of machines, and a nurse scans the various dials and displays, notes something on a clipboard before turning to offer us a smile.

"I'm Nicky. I'll be looking after Mrs Stone for the next few hours."

"Will she be all right?" Declan leans over and peers into the pale features so similar to his own. "I'm Declan. Her son."

"Yes, I recognise you. My boy's a big fan. It's too early to say for sure, but your mother's strong and otherwise in good health." She consults her notes again.

"She's holding her own, the internal bleeding has stopped, which is good news, but there's been some lung trauma, and right now she can't breathe without help. The consultant will be doing her rounds in half an hour, so you can ask her for more details."

Declan murmurs his thanks and takes hold of his mother's hand.

"I'm here, Mum. And Miranda. I have a friend with me, too. Ellie. You'll like her. And Fraze is on his way. He'll be here tomorrow." He turns to the nurse, who is again monitoring the array of devices. "Can she hear me?"

"Maybe. She's been drifting in and out so you never know. We always encourage families to talk to their relatives, and I'll be chatting to her as well."

"I'll go grab a couple more chairs," offers Miranda. "I think it's going to be a long night."

The next five hours tick past. The doctor comes to examine Allannah and explains much the same stuff as Nicky already told us. She does say, though, that Declan's mother is heavily sedated, which is why she's not waking up. Over the next day or so they'll reduce the drugs and she should start to come round. The tube in her throat is a precaution as she's not been breathing too well on her own, but again, once the sedation wears off...

"So, she'll be okay?"

The medic is non-committal. "The next few hours will be crucial. We're monitoring her carefully..."

Declan, Miranda, and the nurse take it in turns to talk to the still figure in the bed. I feel a bit like a spare part but make myself useful fetching coffee from the machine by the main hospital entrance. We're on our third cup when it starts to get light outside, though the blinds remain down on the ward. Intensive care is a strange, timeless world where night and day don't exist and people hover on the very margins of life. Another nurse, Rebecca, takes over from Nicky at nine in the morning, and the doctor appears every couple of hours or so.

By mid-morning, Allannah is starting to stir. She's restless, so Rebecca starts to remove the breathing tube but soon decides to replace it. The nurse smiles at us reassuringly.

"It's good sign that she's trying to breathe on her own. We'll give it an hour or so then try again."

Declan takes hold of Allannah's hand. "Mum, we know you're waking up. Can you hear me?"

A few seconds later he swivels in his chair, his dark, chocolate-coloured eyes wide. "She moved! I'm sure she moved her hand."

Rebecca leans over the bed. "Allannah, can you open your eyes, love? Can you look at me?"

At first there's no reaction.

Rebecca isn't giving up. "Are you awake, love?"

A flicker of her eyelids. Just the briefest movement, but it's there. Allannah opens her eyes, just for a second. Rebecca hits a button to summon the doctor who comes hurrying over.

"What's happening here?"

"She's starting to respond, Doctor. I tried to remove the tube just now, but she was struggling so I left it. Heart rate is near normal, blood pressure, too."

The consultant nods, assessing. She leans over the bed to peel back each eyelid in turn and flashes her slender torch in Allannah's eyes before scanning the notes on the clipboard. "This all looks promising. We could try her with just an oxygen mask. Would you set that up, please?"

The three of us stand in a cluster at the foot of the bed while the doctor removes the tube from Allannah's throat. She starts to gasp for air but soon settles when the mask is placed over her mouth and nose.

"So far so good." The medic checks the monitors and appears satisfied. "Won't be long now."

She's right. It isn't. Less than half an hour later, Allannah opens her eyes again. They are the same dark-brown colour as her son's. It's obvious where he gets his looks from.

"Welcome back, Mum," he murmurs, then he leans over to kiss her cheek. "You gave us quite a scare."

I'm not convinced we're out of the woods yet, but this is definitely a good sign. I stay out of the way as Declan, Miranda, and Rebecca crowd round the bed, but he soon beckons me forward.

"Mum, I want you to meet Ellie." He takes my hand. "Ellie came with me from London."

Allannah regards me with a solemn, steady gaze. Is that the faintest hint of a smile? Difficult to know, behind the mask. Clearly exhausted, she lowers her eyelids, and her breathing deepens.

"She's sleeping," says Rebecca. "You should all do the same. I can call you if anything happens or if there's any news.

Declan shakes his head. "Hathersmuir is an hour's drive away. I prefer to be nearby."

"We could try the Travelodge next door," suggests Miranda. "It's two minutes' walk from the hospital entrance."

Declan still appears doubtful, but Miranda's idea makes sense and, blinking, we troop out into the daylight. My two companions look haggard after a night spent at a hospital bedside, and I doubt I'm any better. We make our way to the budget hotel next door and present ourselves at reception.

The room Declan and I are allotted is okay, plain but functional. The bed looks heavenly. Declan is texting as I dump my clothes on the floor. I assume he's updating Fraze on his mother's condition. I make use of the hotel toiletries to take a quick shower, then I fall into bed, naked and still damp. A few minutes later, Declan crawls in behind me.

"I love you," he murmurs.

"I love you, too, Sir."

CHAPTER TEN

I wake up alone. The room is silent, Declan has already left.

There's a note on the dressing table.

Gone back to the ward. You were asleep, didn't want to wake you. I settled the hotel bill, come over when you're ready.

I check my phone. Ten past four. I feel much more human after a few hours' sleep, though I'm not sure how much rest Declan actually had. I text him.

Just woke up. How is she?

Conscious. Talking.

I offer up a silent thank you to anyone who might be listening. *That's fabulous. Is Fraze there yet?*

No. Due about 5.

OK. See you in half an hour or so.

It actually takes me closer to forty-five minutes to make a cup of tea using the facilities in the room, comb the tangles from my hair after I went to bed with it wet, and shake the wrinkles from my jeans and sweatshirt. Our overnight bags are still in Wilson's boot, so I don't have a change of clothes to hand. When I'm ready, I leave the hotel and make my way back to the hospital.

I arrive at the door to intensive care at the same time as Fraze. He's in business clothes and drags his luggage with him in a small suitcase on wheels so I know he's come here straight from the airport. He dumps his case on the tiled floor and envelopes me in a hug, followed by a deep kiss on the lips.

"You two should get a room."

We split apart and turn to Miranda, who has arrived bearing two cups of coffee, presumably for her and Declan. She looks at me, clearly puzzled. "I thought you and Dec…?"

"I am. I mean, we are…"

"It's a slightly complicated arrangement, but it suits all three of us just fine." Fraze relieves his sister of one of the mugs of steaming latte. "Thanks for this."

I had sort of imagined that Miranda had an idea of how things worked between the three of us, certainly she gave that impression at the wedding, but perhaps I was mistaken. In any case, she is clearly not satisfied with her brother's somewhat sparse explanation, but her priorities are elsewhere for now. She presses the buzzer to request entry to the ward, and we all go in.

Rebecca is hovering beside Allannah's bed making more notes on her clipboard and turns to greet us. "She's improved a lot more since this morning. The doctor thinks we can make plans to move her to another ward soon."

One glance at the patient and I know the nurse is right. Allannah is asleep, but her complexion is less ashen, that awful, deathly wax-like pallor has gone. The oxygen mask still covers her mouth and nose, but several of the blinking, beeping machines have been removed. The bay now looks more like a sickbed and less like the control room for a lunar expedition.

I glance up and down the ward. "Where's Declan?"

"Mrs Stone's son? I'm not sure," replies the nurse. "He was here. They were chatting earlier…"

"Probably taking a leak." Fraze pulls up a seat for his sister, then one for me. "He'll be back soon."

We exchange pleasantries and words of optimism with each other and with Rebecca, but as Allannah shows no sign of waking up the conversation is soon exhausted. After perhaps twenty minutes and no reappearance by Declan, Fraze offers to go and find him.

"Maybe he's in the café," suggests Miranda.

I doubt that. I've been nipping off the ward to text him every two minutes since we arrived here, and he's not answering. If he was just grabbing a sneaky espresso he'd say so. Still, it's as good a place as any to start, so Fraze heads off. He's been gone a couple of minutes when Miranda's phone beeps.

"Sorry, no mobiles in the Unit," admonishes Rebecca.

"I know. I forgot to turn it off. I'll just…" Miranda is already scurrying toward the exit. She returns a couple of minutes later with Fraze. Both appear perplexed.

"Did you find him?" I get to my feet. "What is it? What's happened?"

Miranda answers. "The text was from Stuart. He stayed at home with the boys. He says Dec just showed up at Hathersmuir and he's in a hell of a state."

"What? Why? His mother's doing well. He knows that, doesn't he?" I look to Rebecca for confirmation.

She simply nods. "I would have thought so. They were talking…"

"He wasn't upset," interrupts Miranda, "at least not in that way. According to Stuart, he was boiling mad."

"What? Angry, you mean?" I'm baffled. In the months since Edinburgh, I've never seen Declan irritable, let alone mad. He's one of the calmest people I know.

"What did he talk to his mother about?" Miranda frowns, clearly as nonplussed as I am.

Rebecca shrugs. "I couldn't say, sorry. All I know is he left perhaps half an hour before you arrived. Mrs Stone was exhausted and she's been asleep since, as you know."

I check my phone again despite Rebecca's disapproving scowl. "I've been texting him, but he doesn't answer. I suppose he could have been driving…"

"Driving what?" asks Fraze. "You two flew up here, didn't you? He'll have taken a taxi."

"So he could answer his phone, then."

"Probably. Right, I'm going back to the house to talk to him and find out what's wrong. Miranda, would you mind staying here, with Allannah? I know she's out of danger now, but someone should—"

"Of course," agrees his sister, readily. "I'll let you know if there's any change."

"Thanks." He turns to me. "Ellie, are you coming?"

Too right I am. I slip my hand into Fraze's, and we all but break into a run as we leave the ward.

I have a bad feeling about this.

Fraze flags down a passing taxi in the car park, and we bundle into the rear seat. He gives the driver the address, and we settle in.

"How was your trip? I didn't think to ask you before."

"Fine. I'd just about finished what I needed to do when you texted yesterday."

"But still, you just dropped everything to get back here."

He doesn't answer at once, appears to be thinking, remembering. "My mother wasn't well for years and she died when I was twelve. It was all very harrowing, and Allannah sort of stepped in. She's been like a mother to me and to Miranda. So, yes, I dropped everything. Business is important, but family comes first. And friendship."

"Declan would have needed you. I mean, if his mother hadn't…"

Fraze nods. "He was there for me when I needed someone. They both were. And he would have needed you, too. Thank you for coming with him."

I smile, though my presence doesn't seem to have made much difference.

We're about ten minutes from Hathermuir, and despite the circumstances of my visit, I can't help but gaze in wonder at the scenery. The Highlands are truly stunning, a majestic landscape of purples and yellows and autumnal browns. Shaggy Highland cattle chew on the coarse grass as they contemplate the world going by, clouds scud across the craggy hilltops, and sparkling streams cascade down the steep slopes. Fraze might say he prefers the city, but if I'd grown up here I could never have left it. Picking up on my wonder, he points to a small loch in the distance.

"Fantastic trout fishing there. Would you like to try it?"

"I've never done any fishing."

"Well, this is the perfect place to start. Best salmon and trout in the world, or so my sister keeps telling me."

I suspect he privately agrees.

His phone rings in his suit jacket pocket, and he pulls it out. "Speak of the devil. It's Miranda." He accepts the call. "Hey. Any news?"

A few seconds pass. He listens in silence, his expression grim. "Shit, she really picks her moments. Why did she tell him?" More silence, then, "For fuck's sake…. Did he really not know? Not even an inkling?" He listens to Miranda again, then sighs. "Sounds like he took it badly. Yes, we're almost there. I'll keep you posted."

I wait until he pockets his phone again. "What happened? Was it something about his mother? What did she say?"

He meets my frightened gaze. "From what Miranda can gather, it seems Allannah's near-death experience prompted her to tell Declan about his father. I can only imagine she still thought she might not pull through and wanted to do it while she still could."

"His father? I don't…"

"Allannah never married. It was always just the two of them, though because they lived with us perhaps that wasn't so obvious, at least not to Dec. He never spoke about his father. And I guess his mother didn't, either. Until now."

"And from what you just said, I take it he didn't like what he heard."

He closes his eyes and leans back against the headrest. "I can't believe he really didn't know. I suppose that could explain the tantrum, though, the notion that something so big, so massive, was kept from him."

It's almost as though Fraze is no longer talking to me. His words are for himself, his own private expression of wonder.

An idea occurs to me. I grasp his hand. "Fraze, do you know who Declan's father is?"

He meets my gaze and nods. "Who his father was. He was my father, too. Dec's my half-brother."

Holy Shit! I let out a low whistle. Bloody hell, with bells on.

"Are you sure?" I whisper, though I know he is.

"Oh yes." Fraze gazes out of the car window into the middle distance. "I've known for years. Miranda, too."

"But Declan was in the dark? How could that be? Did no one…?"

"Can you believe we just never talked about it? I think I first began to realise when I was about ten. Even though Dec was, on the face of it, just the son of one of our employees, he always got all the same things I did. A pony, a state-of-the-art bike, skiing in Switzerland, scuba diving off the Great Barrier Reef. He broke his arm once playing football, and my father paid for him to be cared for at a private clinic. He made no distinction between us. Ever."

Fraze drags his fingers through his hair. "I finally knew for sure when my father insisted that Dec was to come to St. Hugh's with me. Not that I minded, Dec was my best friend, and I would never have wanted to leave him behind. But none of it made sense otherwise."

"Why didn't your father just be open about it? It sounds as though he wasn't one to shirk his responsibilities."

"He wasn't. He loved Declan, just like he loved me and Miranda. Everyone could see it, anyone could have joined up the dots. We did."

"But Declan didn't."

"Seems not. When my mother was alive it would have been awkward, to say the least, if it was all brought out into the open, so I always understood why they kept it quiet at first. Then later, Miranda and I sort of took the view that it was Allannah's secret and no one else's business."

"Did they have an affair, then? Declan's mum and your father?"

"At one time, obviously. But I never saw anything to suggest that relationship continued or was ever resumed. Allannah was treated just like an employee—a trusted employee and very close to the family, but no more than that. I don't know the full story because I never asked."

"I can't believe you never spoke to him about it. That it never came up."

"I know, but I didn't. I honestly don't know how I would have raised the subject with Dec, even if I'd wanted to. But why bother? I just sort of shrugged, accepted it, and left well enough alone."

"I can see now why you were always so close."

He nods. "Friends. Brothers. No wonder we both fell for the same woman."

"Lucky you got used to sharing."

Fraze gives a wry chuckle. "Let's hope that extends from submissives to fathers, then. Ah, here we are…"

The car slows down, then turns left to pass through a massive wrought iron gate. The driveway seems to go on forever, but at last we round a slight bend, and the main house comes into view. I gasp. I knew the ancestral home of a duke would be impressive, but not on this scale.

Hathersmuir is simply awesome. A huge, Gothic façade towers over us as the taxi glides to a halt at the foot of the steps leading to the elegant front entrance. The main portion looks to be four storeys high, with only slightly smaller wings extending from the west and the east walls. Turrets on the roofline hint at a past when the house would have been fortified, a safe refuge for the laird and his followers.

"It's beautiful," I breathe. "How old is it?

"The east and west wings were built in the eighteenth century, but the central part dates back to the fifteenth. It would have been much smaller then, though, and a lot of it was destroyed by a fire in the early seventeen hundreds. It was rebuilt to become what you see today."

"How long has it belonged to your family?"

Fraze tosses three twenty-pound notes to the driver, then offers me his hand to help me out of the car. "I'm the seventh duke. The first one was granted the title and the estate in seventeen ninety-three, and it's been ours since then."

As the car pulls away, one half of the huge door opens to reveal a middle-aged woman clad in a tartan skirt made of purple plaid, and a buttoned up green cardigan. She regards us from the top of the steps, her hands folded, and wearing an expression best described as haughty.

"Mrs McBride. I trust you're keeping well." Fraze ascends the stairs to greet her, and I trail after him.

"Your Grace." She inclines her head in a polite bow. "How nice to see you. Mr Ferguson is in the morning room."

"She means Stuart. You'll remember him, from the wedding?"

"Of course. Yes."

"Thank you, Mrs McBride." Fraze extends his hand to me. "This is Ellie Scott, a close friend of mine and Declan's. Speaking of which, where is he?"

"I believe Mr Stone went for a walk in the grounds, sir."

"Right. We'll talk to Stuart, then I'll go and find him."

He starts to tow me past the housekeeper and through the open door. I barely have time to take in the expansive hallway, polished wood furniture, and ornately carved staircase as he tugs me across the gleaming tiled floor.

"Bring us some tea, would you, Mrs McBride? And perhaps some shortbread if you have any."

"At once, Your Grace." She sweeps off to do as he asks.

I'm still getting over 'Your Grace' when Fraze flings open a door about halfway along the hall and marches inside. Stuart is seated at a small table by the French window but he stands up to greet us, a beaming smile on his face.

The men shake hands. Stuart greets me, too, then turns to Fraze again. "Miranda said you were on your way."

Fraze's expression is grim. "So, what happened?"

"Declan arrived in a taxi, thumped on the door to be let in, then stormed past Mrs McBride and me without a word and headed upstairs. When I went after him, he told me to fuck off and offered to toss me over the banister if I didn't get out of his way. There was a lot of door slamming, and as far as I know he went to his apartment. I was busy with the boys so I didn't check. Then, a few minutes later, he slammed back downstairs again and went out. I assume he's still on the estate, though, as no vehicles have gone."

"He didn't say anything?"

"Only what I've told you. He didn't seem to be in a mood for talking."

"Where are the boys now?"

"Dougall took them fishing. Seemed best to get them out of the way…"

Stuart must catch my puzzled expression because he pauses to explain. "Dougall is our ghillie. It's a sort of game keeper. You don't seem to have them in England."

Fraze scrapes his hand across his eyes. "I suppose I'd better go and find him."

"Let him calm down a bit first," suggests Stuart. "Might get more sense out of him, then."

"I doubt it, somehow." Even so, Fraze sinks into a plush, red sofa. "Christ, he could be anywhere. There's over ten thousand acres out there…"

"I wouldn't worry about that," I say. "He's here."

As they've been talking, I've been gazing out of the French windows. I spot a familiar figure emerge from a stand of trees perhaps half a mile from the house, and Declan is now striding towards us.

Fraze stands up. "Well, that saves a lot of time and bother." He opens the French window and steps out onto the terrace beyond.

Stuart and I follow him.

"You wait here," instructs Fraze. "I'll try and make him see reason."

Stuart and I watch in silence as Fraze crosses the expanse of lawn. Stuart speaks first, and he puts into words what I've been thinking.

"I just don't understand why no one ever mentioned any of this to him. It's been an open secret all the time I've known the family, and it's not as though anyone is actually bothered."

"Yes, I know. I get that, but still, I'm not sure why he's so pissed off. And who's he angry with?"

"His mother, I imagine. But he's likely to extend that little circle once he realises that everyone else was in the picture and he wasn't. That they've known for years."

"Oh, God, yes."

Fraze reaches Declan, and even at this distance we can hear raised voices. Declan's doing most of the shouting, but I can't pick out what he's saying. Suddenly Declan swings a punch. He must have taken Fraze by surprise because he staggers back, his hands upraised as though to ward off further attacks. Declan pursues him and swings again, though this time Fraze is ready and ducks. He manages to dodge the next blow, too, but eventually Declan's determined efforts to knock his brother out cold bear fruit and he lands one to his jaw. I have to assume Fraze has had enough of playing nicely and he retaliates. In moments, the pair are swinging punches and rolling across the lawn.

There's a shrill scream. It's me. I sprint over the damp grass, yelling at them to stop. They're going to kill each other, I'm sure of it. Stuart is behind me. We both come to a shuddering halt beside the furious mass of fists, feet, grunts, and Celtic obscenities.

"Stop," I plead. "Please stop."

Tears are streaming across my face as I try to grab first Fraze's jacket, then Declan's T shirt. Stuart, too, does his best, but there's no separating them. Blood pours from Fraze's nose, and Declan's right eye is almost closed. For want of something better to do, I fall to my knees, wailing.

Fraze somehow manages to land a punch to Declan's solar plexus. He curls up, winded, and Fraze takes advantage of the brief respite to roll away from him. He staggers to his feet.

"Shit. I'm sure he broke my nose..."

Declan's only response is a raucous wheezing as he struggles to catch his breath.

I crawl to where he is still rolling on the ground. "Are you all right?"

"He fucking doesn't deserve to be," growls Fraze. "What the fuck was that all about?"

Declan turns his head, his face a mask of fury, of pain and hurt. "You knew." He manages to grind out the words between gasping for air. "You all fucking knew. All those years... I could have...could have..."

Suddenly, without warning, Declan surges to his feet and lunges at Fraze again. Fraze is quicker, though, and has the advantage of already being upright and of being able to breathe. Even so, Declan isn't giving up. I leap up off the grass and without thinking slither between them.

"Ellie, stay out of the way." Fraze tries to move me aside, out of range of any flying fists.

"No. If you're going to fight you'll have to trample over me first."

"Ellie, get out of the way," warns Declan, advancing with murder in his eyes.

"Not a chance." I stand my ground. "I love you. Both of you. You're no good to me without each other, and if you love me like you say you do, you'll find a way to get past this. You have to. Please..."

"Ellie..." Declan's tone is low.

His Dom voice will usually bring me instantly to my knees, but I'm not having it, not this time. Even if they both spank me every day for a month I'm not standing aside to let them kill each other.

"Please," I beg. "Please, Sir. For me..."

Declan hesitates, his features harsh. His dark eyes flash, but not only in anger. There's something else, something more. Something familiar.

"Holy fuck, girl," he growls. "Come here."

I rush into his open arms, and they fold around me. I cling to him, to his neck. He winces when I stroke his bruised cheekbone. Fraze is at my back, his arms also around me, and around Declan, too. Declan stiffens, but he allows it. For long moments the three of us stand there on the lawn at Hathersmuir holding each other upright.

"I'm sorry." Fraze's voice is cracking. "I should have told you, should have said something…"

"I'm not sorry I punched you. I hope your nose is broken, you bastard."

"Well, technically…" begins Fraze but wisely shuts up at the loud throat clearing from Stuart.

"Quite so," offers Stuart from somewhere off to my left. "I think we've given the staff ample entertainment for one afternoon. Perhaps we might all go inside now and discuss this like civilised people. With any luck, Mrs McBride's tea could still be warm…"

CHAPTER ELEVEN

"For years I didn't trust him." Declan sits in the morning room, a cold cup of Mrs McBride's tea before him. He leans forward, his elbows on his thighs and his head down. "I was just the kid of one of his servants, an outsider. I was a hanger-on, but he kept on giving me stuff."

"We noticed," offers Fraze.

Declan bestows a baleful glare on his brother. "He gave you anything you wanted, too. For long enough I assumed I was one of those things, a friend for his precious son and heir, someone for you to play with, a companion. I got cynical, decided to milk the situation, however fucked up it was."

Fraze narrows his eyes. "There was nothing fucked up about it. My father—our father— loved all his children and treated them equally. That included you."

Declan groans. "I can see that now. Sort of. But all the time I was growing up here I thought of him as something of a joke, generous to a fault, but someone I could manipulate. Christ, if I'd known I would have…" He lets his words trail away. "There were times I used to let myself imagine that he was my father, too, but that was just too fantastic, too weird."

"You never said…"

Declan gives a mirthless laugh. "Do you blame me? How would that have sounded? Pathetic or what?"

Fraze doesn't answer. He looks almost as miserable as Declan. For several seconds we sit in silence, Stuart and I making bewildered, helpless eye contact.

Declan gets to his feet. "I loved him. Under all the stupid laddish bravado, I did love him but I never told him that."

"He never said it either, did he?" Fraze remains seated, still dabbing at his nose, though the bleeding has stopped now. "But he showed it, every day. For my father, actions spoke louder than words."

"But I never—"

"He knew. He was never one for talking much, but he would have known."

"We could have been close."

"You were close to him, just as I was."

"And me," Miranda interrupts from the doorway. She enters the room and examines first Fraze's battered features then Declan's. "I see you discussed the matter rationally, then? Like two adults?" She pauses, glances suspiciously at me. "Unless…they weren't fighting over you, were they?"

"No!" We all three answer at once.

She eyes her brothers, then me. "Okay, so…?"

"It was his fault," begins Fraze.

Miranda's response is a disparaging and distinctly unladylike snort. Both her brothers opt to remain silent.

"How is Allannah?" Stuart valiantly attempts to change the subject.

"Worried sick." She fixes her gaze on Declan. "She knows you were upset about what she told you, that you went charging off. That's why I came back, to tell you that you need to go back there and let her see that you're all right. I take it you are all right?"

"I'm getting there," is his grudging response. "I suppose you were in on this little family secret, too?"

"I was, and I can see how that has hurt you. We were wrong. We avoided the issue because it was too awkward, too delicate, and in the process we forgot that you had a right to know. For that, I apologise."

Declan stares at her. I get the impression he didn't expect an apology. I nudge Fraze.

"Yes. Right. I'm sorry, too."

Declan peers at him as though he has sprouted an extra head. "Oh, for fuck's sake… Stop being so humble, both of you. It doesn't suit you at all."

"We'll stop being humble if you stop sulking." Miranda checks the temperature of the teapot before pouring herself a cup.

"I'm not bloody sulking. This is massive. I've a right to be more than a bit pissed off."

Fraze opens his mouth to speak, but it's Stuart who gets in first. "Fair point. No one's arguing with you about that. But they've apologised. I will, too, if it helps. But then you have to let it go. We have to move on."

"What are you talking about? Why the fuck would I—?"

"Because this is your family." Stuart swings his arm to encompass all of us. "They always have been and that's what families do."

Miranda moves across the drawing room to kiss her husband's cheek, then she turns to face Declan again. "This is something we need to talk about, as a family. And we will, in the weeks and months to come. I daresay we all have questions, things we want to say. We should have done it earlier, but what's done is done. You were always stuck with us, Declan, and now you know why." Normally Miranda's imperious bossiness might grate, but her matter of fact attitude is exactly what's required here. She fixes her attention on Declan. "So, are you going back to the hospital or not? Wilson's outside with the car."

He sighs. "Yes, I suppose I should…"

"Go clean yourself up first," I suggest. "There's not much we can do about that black eye, but a shower and some fresh clothes would help. You really don't want to scare your poor mother into a relapse."

"No. And don't you go yelling at her, either," says Fraze. "She's still very fragile, and we won't have you upsetting her. I haven't entirely given up hope that I might be able to lure her back here…"

Declan mutters something suitably obscene and stalks from the room.

"When do you need to get back to London?"

Fraze and I are alone in the formal dining room at Hathersmuir. We are seated at one end of a table that could easily accommodate fifty, though Fraze assures me he can't recall ever seeing that many guests assembled here. We are given to understand that Miranda is considering corporate hospitality as another source of revenue for the estate, and I see no reason to doubt her business sense.

Fraze appears less than impressed, but I've realised by now that Declan was right, Fraze will always criticise and his sister will always listen to what he has to say, ignore him if she chooses, and do what she thinks is best. They understand each other, and the arrangement works well for them.

I cradle my cooling coffee cup in both hands. "I'm expected back at the lab. If not tomorrow, then the day after…"

"Me, too. I have meetings I prefer not to postpone if I can help it. I'm thinking of flying back tomorrow afternoon, depending on how Allannah is, obviously."

"What about Declan?"

Fraze shrugs. "He can probably skip a couple of training sessions. I doubt he'll want to leave here until he's sure she's going to be okay. They were always close. I'm not sure when his next match is. Saturday probably."

"It's only Wednesday. He has a bit of time still…"

Fraze glances at the ornate clock on the mantelpiece, which shows the hour to be just before midnight.

"Is it still Wednesday? Only just." He stands and places his empty cup on the massive sideboard running the length of the room. "Dec'll probably spend the night at the hospital. I'm heading off to bed. What about you?"

I set my cup next to his. "I suppose so. Miranda expects me to use Declan's apartment. I think she had fresh sheets put on the bed."

He gives me his sexy, lop-sided grin. "I see no point in that. Do you?"

"No, but—"

"If Dec comes back he'll know where to look for you. For us."

"What about Miranda?"

"I doubt she'll come looking for you."

"You know what I mean. She's wondering who… Which of you…"

"She'll figure it out, and if she doesn't, Stuart will explain."

"Stuart knows?" I hadn't realized.

Fraze takes my hand and tugs me out into the first-floor hallway. "He doesn't say much, but there's not much gets past our Stuart. Haven't you worked that out yet?"

I'm still processing that snippet as Fraze propels me up another flight of stairs to the second floor.

He and Declan share the east wing—Declan's flat is one floor up from Fraze's. Miranda and her family live in the west wing, and the central façade is the area open to the public or used for formal occasions.

Fraze's apartment is spacious and elegant, though not as comfortable as the flat in Edinburgh or his house in Hatfield. It lacks much in the way of personal items. There are none of the books he likes to keep around him, his sports equipment, his home entertainment. This is not the place where he lives, and he makes no attempt to conceal that.

He shrugs. "Sorry. At least the heating's been on a while…"

"It's fine." And it is fine, by any standards. But it just isn't him.

Fraze is already undressing. He kicks off his shoes, then loses the shirt, still the same one he wore when he flew back from the U.S. and now decidedly crumpled. He balls it up and flings it into a basket, followed by his suit pants and his socks. In just his boxers, he ambles into the adjoining bathroom. Soon I hear the sound of the toilet flushing followed by running water. I peel off my own sweatshirt, jeans, and underwear, and drop them into the basket with Fraze's discarded clothing. I'm not sure where my overnight bag ended up, probably in Declan's apartment, but I'm sure I'll find it tomorrow. Nude, I follow Fraze into the bathroom.

Our eyes meet in the mirror.

He smiles at me. "Christ, you're beautiful."

"You, too, Sir."

He turns, grasps me by the waist, and lifts me up onto the expanse of pearl-coloured marble which surrounds the sink unit. The counter top is cold against my bare flesh, but I don't care. I need this. We need this. I lean back on the tiles behind me while Fraze spreads my legs wide and drops to his knees.

He peels back my already damp folds to expose my clit and hardens his tongue to prod it. He flicks the tip, and I tangle my fingers in his hair to pull him closer, urge him on, beg for more. He shifts, then licks me from my arse right to my clit again. He takes the sensitive bud between his lips and applies suction. I am close to orgasm, already writhing and squirming on the cold surface. I gasp his name, then wail when he suddenly releases me and straightens.

"In the shower," he rasps, shoving his boxers to the floor.

I enter the cubicle, and he hits the control. At once I am doused in cool but rapidly warming water which comes at me from all directions. Fraze follows me in, grabs the shower head from the bracket above me, and adjusts the flow of water through it. The spray is narrowed from the soft sprinkle of droplets to a hard, narrow stream of fast-rushing water. He grasps my leg by the knee and lifts it, opening me. I lean on the smooth, cool wall and try to stifle my cry of pleasure/pain when he angles the torrent of water right at my clit.

There is no preamble, no lead in. The rush of sensation overwhelms me. My leg holding my weight starts to buckle, but Fraze leans forward, pinning me to the tiles in order to continue the relentless assault. I scream, the sound muffled by his shoulder when I shatter. The orgasm is swift and powerful, leaving me gasping under the warm cascade until my senses return.

Fraze lifts me again, and this time I wrap my legs around his waist. I manage to lock my ankles in the small of his back before he drives his cock deep into me. I clench hard, needing him, craving the sense of fullness, of belonging. I want him inside me, moving, taking, reminding me that I am his.

That I am theirs. These friends, now brothers. They share me, and I belong to both.

"He'll be back. Soon." It's as though Fraze hears my thoughts. "He has to come back."

He fucks me hard, his strokes long and deep. I quiver, my arousal swift to peak again, and I wrap myself around him.

"I know," I whisper, moments before we come together.

"Dec? You all right? How's Allanah?"

Fraze's concerned tone rouses me from sleep. I crack open one eye. I am lying beside Fraze in his huge bed, my head resting on his chest. The room is pitch black, and my hair is still damp from the shower. We haven't been asleep for long, it's still the middle of the night. I wince when Fraze reaches for the bedside lamp and turns it on.

Declan is seated on the padded ottoman across the room, his shoulders slumped. His elbows rest on his thighs, his hands dangle between his knees. He eyes the pair of us, though without any rancour or recrimination.

"Is your mum all right," I ask, shoving myself up onto my elbow and pushing the tangled hair from my face.

"Yeah, she's good. Sleeping now."

"You should get some sleep, too," I suggest. "You look knackered."

He manages a twisted smile. "Thanks. I went upstairs, and you weren't there, so…"

"Shall I come with you now?" I start to get out of bed, but Fraze grabs my elbow.

"I've a better idea. Why don't you join us, bro?" He gestures to the space on the other side of where I'm lying. "Plenty of room."

"Here?" Declan waves his arm to the room at large. "We've never—"

"Then it's time we fucking started." Fraze drapes his arm around my shoulders. "I'm not having our Ellie wearing out my ancestral carpet traipsing from my room to yours and back again. Get in."

"It's my ancestral carpet, too," Declan points out, though I note he is already removing his jacket.

"Yeah?" Fraze settles back against the pillows. "Then I assume it'll be your ancestral electricity bill as well. Turn the fucking lights out, will you?"

Three days later, I'm with Fraze and Declan in Fraze's rambling house in Hatfield. Fraze and I caught the flight back from Inverness as planned and came here. Declan followed us a day later, when his mother was released from the intensive care ward.

The place is less the elegant ducal residence, more rustic retreat. A converted barn, it has four bedrooms and three acres of wooded garden and is my favourite of Fraze's three homes. The afternoon is warm, and we are seated on the flagged patio, cool beers on the table before us.

My pussy and arse both throb still from the attention both channels received, first when Declan joined us here last night and again this morning when the three of us awoke in Fraze's bed. I am contentedly satisfied, at least in the physical sense, but I know, too, that something is still bugging Declan. He's quiet, withdrawn, clearly uncomfortable.

Fraze, for all his sharp-tongued humour, is no less attuned to the residual tension between us. He regards Declan with a calm, assessing air.

"You're thinking incest," he announces.

Declan almost chokes on his Belgian lager. "What?" he splutters, before succumbing to a fit of uncontrollable coughing as he tries to clear his airways.

Fraze makes no move to assist his stricken sibling. It's left to me to leap to my feet to slap Declan between the shoulder blades. I glower at Fraze.

"What are you talking about?" I demand. "Are you mad?"

Fraze shakes his head. "No, not mad. But neither am I a man prone to repeating his mistakes. I let important things remain unsaid before, and that didn't work, did it? If there's an elephant in the room, let's be naming it."

"What elephant?" Declan manages to croak the question. "What the fuck…?"

"We were always friends, and now we know we're brothers, right? You and me." Fraze takes another drink from the neck of his bottle. "And we share the same bed. With Ellie, naturally."

"Naturally," agrees Dec, still wheezing. "What would be the fucking point otherwise?"

"Quite. Ellie's what links us, sexually. Nothing else. It's not you and me. It's you and her. And me and her. We share our submissive, because it's the kink we both enjoy."

"We all three enjoy," I correct him.

He acknowledges my remark with a small nod. "I love you, bro. But you know that. You've always known that."

"What is this?" Declan appears bewildered.

"This is me telling it like it is. You and me are close, Dec. We always were, always will be. And now we have Ellie, so in my book that makes things just about fucking perfect. My cock turns solid pretty much every time I look at her. Yours, too?" He pauses, that aristocratic eyebrow raised.

Declan manages a curt nod. "Instant hard-on."

"Right. For her, though. Not for me."

Declan gives a derisive snort. "Of course not for you."

Fraze grins at him. "Don't knock it, mate. There's plenty of guys would find me hot. Still, neither of us is wired that way, so…"

"Right. It's for Ellie. Although knowing that you're there, watching. Touching her, perhaps…"

Fraze chuckles and winks at me as heat flares in my features. "I know. It all adds to the experience. But without Ellie we're just friends. Brothers. If we didn't have her, that's still what we'd be. That's all we'd be. Right?"

"What are you saying?"

"I'm saying nothing's changed, at least not from where I sit. What about you, sweetheart?" He directs his gaze at me.

I shake my head. "No. Definitely not. I love you both. I love this life we have."

And I do. I love it when either or both of them show up in Richmond, or I go to Declan's ultra-modern penthouse in Peterborough or this lovely old place in the heart of rural Hertfordshire. I'm not sure how things will work if…no, when we return to Hathersmuir together, but we'll deal with that when the time comes. I adore the one-on-one fucking which they are both so adept at, but the double Dom relationship is simply mind-blowing. I can't imagine anything else, could never contemplate wanting anything, anyone else.

"What about you?" Fraze fixes his gaze on Declan, deep emerald eyes locked onto dark mahogany ones. "Can you get past the nonsense of the last few days? Get back to where we were? Where Ellie and I still are?" He lowers his voice. "You can see what's at stake."

Long moments pass. Neither wavers, neither breaks eye contact. My gaze is locked on to Declan. He has to be the one to back down, to come around. A part of me, a tiny part, could cheerfully wring Fraze's neck for forcing the issue like this, but a larger part wants the certainty. Either way.

Declan's nod is barely perceptible. I see it and let out a breath I hadn't even known I was holding.

Dark ebony eyes swing from Fraze, to me, then back again. "Okay. But I'm not saying nothing's changed. Some things have. Or will. But not this. Not us."

Fraze finishes his beer and gets to his feet. "Fair enough. Glad we got that settled. Another beer?"

CHAPTER TWELVE

I'm writing up some notes in my lab when my mobile rings. I glance at the display.

Declan.

I hit 'accept'. "Hi. How are you?"

"I'm good. My mum just phoned. She's coming home tomorrow."

"Really? That's wonderful."

Allannah has been on a normal ward for the last ten days, and despite the reassurances from the hospital staff, I know Declan has fretted about her. He's made two return visits to Inverness when he could shoehorn the trip into his playing and training schedule but mostly he's had to rely on updates from Miranda.

"Is she going to Hathersmuir or her cottage?"

"She still has her arm in plaster and has to use a wheelchair so it'll be Hathersmuir at first. Fraze and I thought we'd go up there, spend a few days."

"Want company?"

"We were hoping you'd say that. There's a flight first thing in the morning."

"Shall I book the tickets?"

"I already did. Can you get to Heathrow for six-thirty?"

"I'll see you there."

Wilson met us at the airport, but Fraze and I hopped in a taxi for the drive to Hathersmuir, while Declan took the limo and headed into the city to accompany his mother back from the hospital.

We've been awaiting their arrival in the drawing room at Hathersmuir.

"They're here." Miranda pops her head around the door. "I just spotted the car from the landing window." She hurries on across the hall in the direction of the front door, throws that open, and goes out onto the top step.

Fraze, Stuart, and their two boys follow Miranda outside, so there's quite a welcoming committee assembled to greet the car as Wilson pulls up outside. Fraze jogs down the steps to open the car door and help the ex-housekeeper out.

Allannah's right arm is in a sling and she sinks gratefully into the wheelchair which Declan produces from the car boot. Still, there's no mistaking the beaming smile as she looks up at the facade of Hathersmuir.

Fraze doesn't miss it, either. "Welcome home, Allannah." He kisses her cheek. "Your old apartment's all ready for you."

He means the spacious flat she used to occupy when she worked here, the one which, in theory at least, Declan still uses on the rare occasions he returns to the Highlands. In practice the three of us will share Fraze's apartment.

"Thank you. It's really very kind of you to let me come back here to recuperate."

"Where else would you go? This is your home. It always has been." Miranda jostles Fraze aside so she can also drop a kiss on Allannah's cheek. "Do you want to go straight up there, get some rest, perhaps?"

"I've been resting for the best part of three weeks. I don't suppose there's a nice cup of tea to be had, is there?"

"Mrs McBride will bring a tray to the drawing room." Miranda beckons to her brothers. "You two can manage the wheelchair up the steps, can't you?"

A few minutes later, with the exception of the two boys who are again going fishing with the ghillie, we're all seated in the elegant drawing room, the sunlight dappling the carpet through the French window. Allannah looks about her.

"I see you moved the Lowry." She is scowling at the beautiful landscape painting above the main fireplace

"Yes," agrees Miranda. "It's in the library now. We thought the Gainsborough looked better in here."

In the weeks I've spent at Hathersmuir, I've become accustomed to the family bandying around the names of great artists whose works hang on the walls. Apparently, the old duke was a renowned collector. I've also gotten used to the notion that we have a drawing room, and a library, and even a great ballroom on the first floor, though Fraze insists it's intended for ball games such as cricket.

Allannah purses her lips. "The chandelier in the hallway needs cleaning."

"I'll mention it to Mrs McBride," Miranda promises. "It is still just one lump of sugar, isn't it?"

"Thank you, yes." Allannah takes a sip of her tea and nods her approval. At least Mrs McBride is not found wanting here. She takes another drink then sets her cup down on the saucer. "I'm glad we're all together. I was hoping for a chance to explain…"

"There's no need. Really."

It's as though Fraze never spoke.

Allannah continues. "It was all a long time ago now, of course. But you have a right to know."

When Miranda would have interrupted, Allannah waves her good hand at her. "Please, let me finish…"

Miranda subsides, and we all sit in silence, waiting.

Allannah furrows her brow as though gathering her thoughts. "I was just eighteen and working as a waitress in Glasgow. I'd not long moved over here from Clarinbridge. That's in County Galway. There were no jobs in Ireland, so…"

Fraze gets to his feet and goes to stand by the window. "Is that where you met my father, then? In Glasgow?"

"Yes. I worked behind the bar in a hotel, and he was staying there. He asked for a whisky, and I told him the Lyons was best. He laughed and said I was dead right there. We got chatting, and one thing led to another." She gazes off into space. "He was good company…"

"Did you love him?" asks Miranda.

Allannah considers that for a few moments. "Maybe, a little. For a while at least. Long enough to…well, you know…" She gives a wry laugh. "It was only a temporary thing, we both knew that. He was married, he had responsibilities, a family. He made no secret of it, and I was too young and silly to care."

She paused to meet Miranda's assessing gaze. "I'm not proud of that, it was wrong, I know. But he was nice to me, we had fun. Then his business in Glasgow was done, and he left the hotel. A few weeks later, I realised that I was expecting."

She reaches for the teapot, but Miranda beats her to it.

"Let me."

Her cup replenished, Allannah resumes her story. "I knew who he was, obviously. I knew about Hathersmuir, his family home. So, I wrote him a letter. I explained the predicament I was in and asked him for money. I thought ten thousand pounds would be enough to set me up, see me through the pregnancy and birth, and make sure me and the baby had a place to live, food. Babies are expensive, and it wasn't a lot, not to him. I half expected him to refuse, to say there was no proof the baby was even his. There would have been nothing I could have done…"

"I take it he didn't refuse."

Alannah glances up at Fraze. "No. He gave me the money, all ten thousand pounds of it. He also offered me a job and a home. Here." She flutters her hand. "Of course, I refused, it just seemed weird. Sort of awkward. We were a fling, it wasn't meant to wreck his marriage or tie us to each other for life. But he came looking for me in Glasgow. He handed me the cheque for the money but convinced me to at least try his suggestion until the baby was born. So, I did. I reckoned I had nothing to lose, and I didn't want to be pregnant and on my own. Going back to Ireland was quite out of the question, so I came back here with your father as assistant cook. It was a decent job. I had a nice room and my board, and when I needed it, I had time off. He insisted I go to a lovely private hospital to give birth, the same one your mother went to. I was very well looked after. He even came to see me while I was there. He brought you, Miss Miranda, though you won't remember. You were very tiny…"

Allannah smiles, the recollections obviously pleasant. "A few weeks after Declan was born, I was told I could leave my baby with the family nanny if I wanted to while I went back to my duties in the kitchen. If the other staff or the duchess thought it odd, no one said anything. He was the duke, you see, and he said I could stay."

"Yes, he could be pretty forceful when he wanted to be," agrees Miranda.

Allannah nods. "You were just a little girl then, perhaps four years old. And your brother was born six months after my Declan, so they were always playmates. They were brought up together, in the nursery here at Hathersmuir, then they went to school together. Meanwhile I went to college. I got qualifications in catering so I could support myself and my little boy. I might have moved on, I could have, but there was never any pressure to do that. Declan was happy, and I was offered the job of cook when old Mrs Flynn retired. It was the duchess who promoted me."

"Did our mother know? About you and…?"

Allannah nods. "I'm certain she did. But she was no fool. She also knew that her husband loved her, not me. I was no threat, and although at times she seemed cold and distant, she was never vindictive. She seemed content to let me stay here as long as I didn't flaunt the fact that her husband fathered my son. So I didn't. I kept my head down, did my best to be a good employee. I enjoyed the work. I was happy here. Then, when the duchess passed away, it seemed I couldn't leave even if I'd wanted to. I was needed at Hathersmuir, and I felt I owed it to the family to stay, to do what I could to help…"

"No one could have done more. I don't know how we'd have managed without you." Fraze strides back from the window to crouch in front of his old housekeeper. "I loved my mother, don't get me wrong about that, and I missed her. But even when she was alive, you were always a hell of a lot warmer. You were always the one to go to with cut knees or broken toys."

Miranda reaches for Allannah's uninjured hand. "You made a ball dress for my Sindy doll. And you were the one I came to the day I started my periods."

"Well, of course. Who else—?"

"We knew all along. About you and our father. We knew Declan was our half-brother."

"I wondered. I was never sure… I didn't want anyone to be hurt."

"We weren't."

"And your mother? What about the duchess?"

Miranda flattens her lips, thinking. Her response is a while in coming. "From what you say, it sounds as though she learned to live with it. The fact that you never flaunted your relationship, never forced her to confront it, probably helped."

"There was no relationship, not after that first time. I worked here, that was all. I was staff."

Fraze shakes his head. "You were always a lot more than that, Allannah. You both were, you and Dec. You must know that. That's why our father left Lyons Whisky to Declan, the most lucrative of his businesses, not tied to the estate. That distillery makes a fortune. It was his way of providing for his son. Your cottage, too, and your pension. He was making sure you'd always have a roof over your head, always be comfortable. Not just staff, not by a long chalk."

"I was worried that you might resent it, your father's generosity."

"There was always enough to go round, and we got used to sharing our toys as we grew up."

He catches my eye, then Declan's. I flush scarlet as Miranda clears her throat. I imagine Stuart has had a word by now.

"Would anyone like any more tea?"

We all decline, so Mrs McBride is summoned to clear the tray away.

"Shall I help you upstairs?" offers Declan. "You know, Fraze got a lift installed."

"You didn't! For me?"

"Of course for you." Fraze grasps the handles of the wheelchair. "Nothing but the best." He wheels her toward the door. "Just staff, indeed…"

I hesitate at the door to Fraze's room. He's here, as I knew he would be. Declan, too, and the pair of them are deep in conversation. The dark head and the pale blond one are close as they speak softly, earnestly. They pause and look over at me, framed in the doorway.

Suddenly self-conscious and unsure, I make to retreat. "Sorry. I didn't mean to disturb you…"

"No, come in." Fraze smiles at me. "We were just talking about you."

I feared as much. And whatever they were saying, it's serious and I'm pretty sure I don't want to hear it. I inhale deeply, then step forward into the room and close the door behind me with a gentle click. "Is something wrong?" I ask.

Fraze furrows his brow. "Not wrong, exactly. But we've been discussing our…arrangement and we'd like to make some changes."

"Changes," I echo, my heart sinking. Is this it? The moment when they explain, gently but firmly, that I don't fit in here, at Hathersmuir. That this is their world, not mine? I look from one to the other, and I wait.

Declan wanders across to the huge four-poster bed and perches on the end of it. "These last few weeks…" he begins, his gaze on his shoes. He raises his eyes to meet mine. "There's been so much upheaval, a lot has changed. Relationships shifting, things we took for granted…"

My mouth goes dry, but I will myself not to interrupt. If they want rid of me they'll have to say so.

"We were thinking we might…" Declan pauses, not breaking eye contact with me, "… we might clarify matters somewhat."

"Clarify?" I'm sounding like a parrot.

"Clarify," Declan confirms. "With a collar."

"A co—"

"We talked about this once before, a while ago." Fraze interrupts and comes to stand close to me. He trails his fingertip around the front of my throat. "Do you remember?"

"Yes," I whisper. "It was on the train, when we left Edinburgh that first time. You mentioned commitment."

"That's right. You didn't say anything then, and it was early days. We let it go, but it's been a few months now. We want you to consider it."

"Consider what?" I narrow my eyes at him. He'll have to spell this out. "What are you asking, exactly?"

Fraze cups my chin in his palm and angles my face towards his. "We want you to accept our collar, make this thing between us official. Well, as official as a collaring ceremony can be. It has meaning for us, though."

"Like a marriage?"

"Almost exactly like a marriage, except our approach is more flexible. It can include three people, to start with. It's a big step, an act of faith and trust for us and for the people who we invite to witness it."

"Witnesses?" My mind is racing, not quite over the awful shock of initially thinking they wanted to end it with me. "Who would we invite?"

Ashe Barker

Declan takes over. "The people who matter to us. Close family, of course. Friends, if we trust them. You know that both Fraze and I like to keep our lifestyle low profile, so we're not thinking of a large affair. It would be very low-key, definitely private. My mother would be there. And Miranda and Stuart."

"Do they know about us? I mean, Miranda and Stuart, yes, but what about your mother?"

Declan shrugs. "She's not daft. She'll have an idea, and she'll be all right with it. She likes you."

"I like her, too. But...I can't believe they'd all just accept such an arrangement. I mean, the dukedom, all of this..." I wave my arm to indicate the room, and beyond that the huge stately home, steeped in tradition, in expectation, in a sense of how things should be done.

Fraze shakes his head. "Surely you've realised by now that we don't give a fuck about any of that. My family, our family, has spent at least the last couple of generations keeping up appearances but doing exactly what we liked, what makes us happy, what works for the people who matter. My father did that, my mother, too. So did Allannah when she decided it suited her to stay here rather than move on after Dec was born. It's there in the arrangement I have with my sister, which means she has Hathersmuir, the home she loves, the place she understands, and I have my freedom to live where and how I please. Miranda runs the estate better than I ever could. It's in her bones, and she'll pass it on to her sons with my blessing. This thing between us, this lifestyle we're choosing, it's no different. We'll make room for it, find ways to make it work."

"You're serious, aren't you? You really mean it. You want this. You want me."

Declan's dark-chocolate eyes are heated as he regards me with the utmost seriousness for once. "We do. We absolutely do. So, is there anyone you'd want to invite?"

"I'm not sure. I mean..."

"She hasn't even agreed to the collaring yet," puts in Fraze.

"No, you're right." Declan flashes me an apologetic grin. "Sorry, I didn't mean to rush you. It's a big decision. You'll have questions, concerns..."

I consider that for a few moments. "Actually, I don't. Well, not many." I manage to find my voice at last. "I... I think I understand what a collaring ceremony is. What it would mean."

"Do you?" Declan cocks his head, one dark eyebrow raised.

Fraze chuckles. "Of course she fucking does. Our Ellie's a researcher. She does it for a living. You've been ferreting out information on collaring ceremonies, haven't you?"

"I have, yes."

Fraze has hit the nail on the head. As soon as the idea was planted all those months ago, my curiosity was piqued. I was keen to know more, to understand the significance of the concept. So, I reverted to type and looked it up. I trawled the internet for a couple of evenings collecting articles, blog posts, any information I could find about BDSM collaring. I think it's fair to say I'm pretty well-informed. I know exactly what I'd be letting myself in for. I shift my gaze from one to the other. "Is that what you want? Both of you?"

Their faces are solemn, serious. Declan speaks for both of them. "We do want it. Very much."

I manage a tremulous smile as tears threaten. "I want it, too."

Declan seizes me around the waist and swings me into the air before planting a hard kiss on my lips. Then Fraze grabs me and does much the same. I'm dizzy, my head reeling by the time we all three tumble onto the bed.

"You do realise that if — when — you wear our collar you'll be ours. Forever." Fraze props himself up on his elbow to peer down at me.

"I know that."

"You'll be obedient. Which means you strip on command."

"Yes, Sir. Shall I do that now?"

"In a moment," says Declan. "We might insist that you call us 'Master'. And kneel when one of us comes into the room."

"I've never done that."

"No, but we can work on it. Can you do that, Ellie?" There's a wicked gleam in his eye.

Is he serious?

I'm taking no chances. "I… I think I can. I want to try."

"Good enough."

"Will I have to live in one of your houses?"

Fraze looks at Declan, then back at me. "Not necessarily. We thought we'd keep all our places on. Your flat's convenient for when we want to be in the city, and for your work. You won't be giving that up, will you?"

"I don't want to, no. But…"

"You're good at what you do. And it's important work. We don't expect you to stop. Our relationship will be a private one, our public and professional lives will remain much the same, but we all know we're together. It's us, we three and no one else. The collar symbolises that. It says you belong to us, but it's our responsibility to make you happy, to ensure you have all you need. And you need your work. Don't you?"

"Yes. I do."

"Right, then. You can strip now."

I scramble up to kneel on the mattress between them and start to unfasten my blouse. "Where would the ceremony take place?"

Fraze answers me. "We thought here. There's no point having a house that doubles as a wedding venue and not taking advantage of it. The ballroom is the usual place for this sort of thing. Miranda decks it out with lace drapery, flowers, pretty pink covers for the chairs.

"Pink covers? Hardly!" Declan's distaste is writ plain across his gorgeous features. "And I think we could give the lace a miss, too."

I tend to agree. "Maybe, since it will be a small affair, we could just have a few candles. Flowers might be nice…"

Declan nods, looking relieved. "Flowers, then. And candles. Is there anyone you'd want to have there, Ellie? Your father, perhaps?"

I gulp. "I'm not sure. I mean, he knows about you. Last time I was in Leeds I told him I was seeing you, both of you. It's fair to say he was a bit puzzled, but he didn't say much or ask many questions. I don't think he realises how serious we are…"

"Do you want him to see that? To know the truth about how it is between the three of us?"

I nod. "If I'm to be married, or as close to it as I'm ever likely to come, I can't do that without him there. Since my mother died, I'm all he has. He'd be so hurt if I didn't include him, he'd never understand why…"

"Then we need to go and see him. We'll mount a charm offensive." Fraze treats me to another of his sexy grins as I peel my skirt down and kick it away from the bed. "I can be very charming when the occasion calls for it." He jerks his thumb in Declan's direction. "And he'll do his best."

EPILOGUE

"Thank you for being here." I turn my head to smile at my father.

He stands at my side in his finest suit, pride beaming from his face as he returns my smile. "Where else would I be? My daughter, my only daughter, is getting married."

"Not married, Dad. I explained…"

"You did, but I confess I'm still baffled." He squeezes my hand. "I'm an old-fashioned guy, I suppose. If your mother was alive she'd understand it, I daresay."

Personally, I doubt that. His utter bewilderment in the face of all of this makes my dad's presence here all the more precious to me. "I'm so glad you came. I wasn't sure if you would."

"I said so, didn't I?"

"Yes, but—"

"Look at me, Eleanor." His tone is firm now, the voice he used to use when I misbehaved as a child.

I tilt my chin to meet his steady gaze.

"They're fine young men, both of them. I think it's fair to say you hit the jackpot there, though I don't have a clue how you ended up marrying both. I won't pretend to know how it's all going to work, but it's enough for me to hear you say that it will, that this is truly what you want. I've always trusted you. This is all a bit beyond me, but one thing I do know, and that's what happiness looks like. I had it with your mother, and I see it now, when I look at you."

He lifted a hand to stroke her cheek. "You're glowing, my love, and if your duke and your footballer can do that for you, then I've no quarrel with either of them. Your mother would have said the same."

"I love you, Dad."

"And I love you. I'm the proudest man here, do you know that?"

"Thank you," I whisper.

He wraps his arm around my shoulders and squeezes me tight. "Stop thanking me. I'm your dad, you can take me for granted. Anyway, I think it's just about time for us to go in."

Fraze, Declan, and I discussed the type of ceremony we ought to have and opted to design our own. We decided on something simple and short, modelled on a traditional wedding ceremony. So, my dress is white, though with no lace since Declan apparently loathes the stuff. I settled for a swathe of pale silk, and I love the way it drapes around my hips. The neckline is low but not provocative, and the bodice is decorated with small bows. The whole thing laces up the back, corset-style. I wear no jewellery, but I do carry two roses in my hand. Despite the valiant efforts of the saleswoman in the bridal shop, I didn't purchase a veil or headdress. My hair is secured in a small knot at the back of my head. Miranda helped me to pin it up after she'd laced me into my gorgeous gown.

We agreed on a guest list of just four—Miranda, Stuart, Allannah, and my father. Miranda's boys are away for the weekend, and to avoid any unwelcome attention, the servants have been given time off. The only one to remain is Mrs McBride who insists upon cooking and serving us a meal to celebrate this special event. The plan is to sit down together in the dining room after the formal part of the gathering is concluded.

Everyone else is already assembled. I am to enter last, with my father. He insisted he wanted to walk me down the aisle, or the Hathersmuir ballroom equivalent of it, so we wove that into the ceremony. We stand at the closed door, ready to make our entrance.

"Ready?" He looks to me for my signal.

I nod, and he reaches for the door handle.

Music is playing, the soft, muted melody of Stanley Myers' Cavatina. I halt in the doorway to take in the scene.

Ashe Barker

Fraze and Declan face me from the far end of the huge room, flanked by Allannah, Miranda, and Stuart. Formally dressed, Fraze in his traditional family tartan and Declan in a crisp, grey suit, my two Doms have never looked more handsome, never sexier, never more forbidding than they do in this moment. My stomach clenches, my pussy tingles. If this dress would permit underwear it would be damp. I swallow hard.

"Sweetheart?" My father extends his elbow, and I slide my hand into the crook of it. He takes a pace forward, and I match his step.

We walk the length of the ballroom, our progress slow, measured. I'm glad of my father's calm, his strength. I could never have done this alone. We reach the silent group waiting for us. My father relinquishes my hand and moves to the side to stand next to Allannah.

I face Fraze and Declan, and the music dies away. The room is silent for a few moments, then I slowly drop to my knees before my two Doms. I hold my head straight but lower my gaze to the polished floor.

Long moments pass as I wait for the ceremony to commence.

"Do you offer us your love?" Fraze speaks first.

"I do, Sir. I offer my love to you." My heart is thumping. I'm so nervous I can barely speak. My voice sounds breathy as I try to say my words clearly.

Declan speaks next. "Do you offer your love to both of us, unconditionally?"

"I do, Sir. I swear it."

"Do you offer us your submission and your obedience?"

"I do, Sir. I swear to obey each of you, and to submit to your control, both individually and together."

"Do you do so of your own free will? Do you choose to belong to us?"

"I do, Sir."

"And do you bring a symbol to demonstrate that commitment?"

"I bring you each a rose, Sir, to signify my love and my respect, and my lifelong submission." I hold out the two red roses, and they each take one to attach to their lapels.

Declan continues the ceremony. "We thank you for your gifts. This collar symbolises our ownership of you, and our lifelong commitment to take care of you, to control your life with respect and love, and to do all in our power to ensure your happiness and wellbeing."

He turns to pick up the collar, which has been on a table behind them. I'm excited, eager to see it, but I know that my part in this ritual involves not looking up until I am given permission to do so. I keep my eyes lowered when Declan bends to place the collar around my bare neck.

The metal is cool against my skin, but the piece feels light. His fingers brush the nape of my neck as he fastens the collar, then Fraze leans in to secure a second clasp. They straighten, then Declan lays his hand on the top of my head.

"You may look up now."

I do, and my pussy clenches. They are so sexy, so stern, so impossibly gorgeous. And so mine.

Fraze also places his palm on my head. "You belong to us now, our submissive. Never forget the honour and respect we have for you. You have submitted willingly to our care and control, and should it be required, to our discipline. We promise to take our responsibilities seriously, to always treasure the gift of your submission, as it deserves. We will endeavour to always be worthy of the trust you have shown us today."

They both extend a hand, and I place my palms in each of theirs. They draw me to my feet. Fraze kisses me first, a chaste peck on my cheek. Declan follows suit, then grasps me around my waist and hugs me to him.

"Loving the dress," he growls before sliding his lips across mine.

Fraze swings me about to face him and plants a much more suggestive kiss on my lips. "Me, too," he agrees, "though you'll look even better without it."

"For Heaven's sake, put the girl down." Allannah bats Fraze's hands away. "Let me look at her. Oooh, that's beautiful." She trails her fingers along my new collar. "It's gold, I can see that, and platinum."

"Nothing but the best for our Ellie," confirms Fraze. "Dec designed it, and we had it made in Edinburgh."

Allannah links her arm in mine. "Welcome to the family, my dear."

Miranda does her own inspection of my collar. "It really is exquisite." She turns to my father. "Don't you think so, Mr Scott?"

"Please, call me Harry." My dad still looks slightly stunned by the whole affair but is already beaming and shaking hands, first with Declan, then Fraze.

Stuart is busily pouring drinks for everyone and proposes a toast. "To happy families," he announces to the room at large when we are all supplied with a flute of sparkling champagne.

We return the toast and toss back the champagne, then Miranda takes my other arm. "Such a lovely ceremony, very moving. It was perfect, quite perfect."

I have to agree.

Miranda steers me towards the door. "Shall we go down to the dining room? I believe Mrs McBride has outdone herself…"

The rest of the group follow us, still exchanging congratulations. I want to pinch myself but resist the urge. Sometimes, however strange, however impossible, dreams do come true.

FROM THE AUTHOR

Thank you for reading *Her Two Doms*. If you enjoyed the story, I would really appreciate it if you would leave a review. Reviews are invaluable to indie authors in helping us to market our books and they provide useful feedback to help us work even harder to bring you more of the stories you love.

ABOUT THE AUTHOR

USA Today best-selling author Ashe Barker has been an avid reader of fiction for many years, erotic and other genres. She still loves reading, the hotter the better. But now she has a good excuse for her guilty pleasure – research.

Ashe lives in the North of England, on the edge of the Brontë moors and enjoys the occasional flirtation with pole dancing and drinking Earl Grey tea. When not writing – which is not very often these days - her time is divided between her role as taxi driver for her teenage daughter, and caring for a menagerie of dogs, tortoises. And a very grumpy cockatiel.

At the last count Ashe had around sixty titles on general release with publishers on both sides of the Atlantic, and several more in the pipeline. She writes M/f, M/M, and occasionally rings the changes with a little M/M/f. Ashe's books invariably feature BDSM. She writes explicit stories, always hot, but offering far more than just sizzling sex. Ashe likes to read about complex characters, and to lose herself in compelling plots, so that's what she writes too.

Ashe has a pile of story ideas still to work through and keeps thinking of new ones at the most unlikely moments, so you can expect to see a lot more from her.

Ashe loves to hear from readers. Feel free to follow her on social media or visit her website at www.ashebarker.com

Or you can email her direct on ashe.barker1@gmail.com

Better still, sign up for Ashe's newsletter to be the first to hear about new releases, competitions, giveaways and other fun stuff. The link is on her website.

ALSO BY ASHE BARKER

Contemporary
* Broken
  Highland Odyssey
  Above and Beyond
  Capri Heat
* The Master (with Katy Swann)
* Making The Rules
* Faith
* Spirit
* Hardened
* Tell Me
* First Impressions
* Dark Melodies
* Sure Mastery
* Hard Limits
* Laid Bare
* The Three Rs
* Chameleon
* La Brat
* Red Skye at Night

Historical
* Her Celtic Masters
* Conquered by the Viking
* Her Rogue Viking
* Her Dark Viking
* Her Celtic Captor
* The Duke and the Thief (with Jaye Peaches)
* The Widow is Mine (The Conquered Brides collection)
* A Scandalous Arrangement
* The Highwayman's Lady
* Her Noble Lords
* The Laird and the Sassenach
  Sassenach Bride

Sci-fi
* Her Alien Commander
* Theirs: Found and Claimed

Paranormal and Time Travel
- Shared by the Highlanders
- Held In Custody
  Under Viking Dominion
- Resurrection

LGBT
- Gideon
- Bodywork
- Hard Riders

Short Stories and Novellas
- Rough Diamonds
- Re-Awakening
- Carrot and Coriander
- Right of Salvage
- In the Eyes of the Law
- The Prize
- A Very Private Performance
- Yes or No?
- Rose's Are Red

Made in the USA
Middletown, DE
10 September 2020